Morality
Play

BARRY UNSWORTH

Morality

Play

NAN A. TALESE */ - 2594*

DOUBLEDAY

New York   London   Toronto   Sydney   Auckland

PUBLISHED BY NAN A. TALESE
an imprint of Doubleday
a division of Bantam Doubleday Dell Publishing Group, Inc.
1540 Broadway, New York, New York 10036

DOUBLEDAY is a trademark of Doubleday, a division of
Bantam Doubleday Dell Publishing Group, Inc.

First published in the United Kingdom by Hamish Hamilton, Ltd., London

Book design by Paul Randall Mize

Library of Congress Cataloging-in-Publication Data

Unsworth, Barry, 1930–
Morality play/Barry Unsworth.—1st ed. in the U.S.A.
p.   cm.
1. Great Britain—History—14th century—Fiction.
2. Catholic Church—Clergy—England—Fiction.
3. Theater—England—History—Fiction.   I. Title.
PR6071.N8M67   1995
823′.914—dc20   95-4106
CIP

ISBN 0-385-47953-0
Copyright © 1995 by Barry Unsworth
All Rights Reserved
Printed in the United States of America
November 1995

5   7   9   10   8   6   4

Morality
Play

One

IT WAS A DEATH that began it all and another death that led us on. The first was of the man called Brendan and I saw the moment of it. I saw them gather round and crouch over him in the bitter cold, then start back to give the soul passage. It was as if they played his death for me and this was a strange thing, as they did not know I watched, and I did not then know what they were.

Strange too that I should have been led to them, whether by angels or demons, at a time when my folly had brought me to such great need. I will not hide my sins, or what is the worth of absolution? That very day hunger had brought me to adultery and through adultery I had lost my cloak.

I am only a poor scholar, open-breeched to the winds of heaven as people say, with nothing but Latin to recommend me, but I am young and well favored though short of stature and women have looked at me sometimes. Such a thing had befallen not much before I saw Brendan die, though in this case, as I have said, it was not lust but hunger drove me,

a lesser sin, I was hoping she would give me to eat, but she
was too hasty and hot. Then by ill luck the husband returned before expected and I had to escape through the
cowshed and left my good cloak behind in that bitter December weather. I was in fear of pursuit and broken bones,
though it is forbidden to strike a man in Holy Orders, and
so I was walking at the edge of the woodland and not on the
open road. If I had kept to the road I would have passed by
without seeing them.

There was a clearing, a place where a track led from the
road into the wood. They had brought their cart here and
I came upon them as they were taking the man down. I
watched from among the trees without making it known. I
was afraid to come forward. I thought they were robbers.
They wore pieces of clothing that were strange and ill-
assorted and seemed not to belong to them. These are dangerous times and a cleric is forbidden to bear weapons, all I
had was a short stick. (Sticks, clubs, and cudgels, being
without point or cutting edge, naturally do not come under
the ban.)

From my place in hiding I saw them bring him down
from the cart, the gaunt, half-grown hound that was with
them jumping up eagerly as if in play and showing his pale
tongue. I glimpsed the man's face with the shine of death on
it. They laid him down there in the open. They had brought
him there to be close to his death, I understood this also at
the same moment. For who would wish to see a companion
gasp his last on a jolting cart? We desire to keep the dying
and the newly dead close before our eyes so as to give them
full meed of pity. Our Lord was brought down to be pitied,
on the Cross He was too far away.

They crouched around him in a circle, huddling close as if
he were a fire to give warmth to them on this winter day, six
persons—four men, a boy, and a woman. They were
dressed in cast-off scraps and pieces against all regulation of

clothing for the people, one in a green hat with a plume to it such as the rich wear though he was poorly enough clad otherwise, another wore a white smock to the knees with his threadbare hose showing below, another—the boy—a lumpy shawl of what seemed horsehair. The oaks beyond them had some russet still, last year's foliage dry on the stalk, and there was a gleam of light on it and on the coarse pelt of the boy's shawl. The man was dying unshriven, there might have been time to hold out the Cross to him, but I was afraid to approach. *Mea maxima culpa.*

I could not see him now but I could hear across the space that separated us the struggle of his breath and I could see the mist of breath from the mouths of those above him. This was like incense, a fume of devotion. Then the sound ceased and I saw them shift back to make space for Death, a thing very wise to do, Death being less provoked when at large than when confined. It was like that scene in the Morality Play when the besieged soul flies free at last. It was then I saw that one of the men had a badge of livery, the emblem of a patron sewn to his cap.

It was then too that the dog found me out. This was a half-starved beast with every rib visible but it showed neither fawning nor cringing, merely an ignorant goodwill. It had attempted more than once to break into the circle around the dead man and being repulsed had then gone snuffling at the edges of the clearing and so finally came upon me crouched behind my tree and fell to yapping, more it seemed in welcome than threat, and this brought one of the men, he of the green hat, a hulking, ragged fellow with black hair tied behind and eyes black as damson, who drew a knife at the sight of me, and when I saw this I got to my feet with all haste and made the openhanded priestly gesture of gratitude for blessing—this so he should see at once what I was. "Come forth and show your face," he said.

At this I came forward promptly enough. "I was walking

through the trees," I said. "I came upon you by accident. I was unwilling to interrupt at such a moment."

They had started up from the dead man, whose eyes were wide open and blue as a thrush's egg. He was bald and round-headed, with a blubbery face like a mask of lard and his mouth was crooked and hung open a little at the lower end. The cur took advantage of the diversion to lick at his face and this licking pulled the mouth more open. The boy kicked the dog and it yelped and went and pissed against a tree. "A priest," the boy said. It was not a shawl that he wore over his shoulders, but some sort of garment with trailing leg pieces. I saw now that he was weeping—his face was wet with tears.

"You might have gone back or taken another way," the one with the badge in his cap said. "You chose to spy." The emblem was a white stork above crossed halberds. I knew this man for the leader because of the badge, also because he spoke for them all. He was some years older than I, of middling height, slender of body but wiry and quick. He alone had no borrowed clothes about him. He wore a jerkin of sheepskin with a short tunic below it much frayed at the neck. The muscles in his calves and thighs showed prominently through the thin stuff of his hose. "You came too late even to do your office," he said with contempt. "Brendan died with his sins upon him while you were skulking there." His face was a narrow oval, white now with grief or cold. The eyes were beautiful, gray-green in color, set below slanting brows. Later I was to wonder why I saw no danger in this zealot's face of his, but my divining soul was lost in the fear of the moment. I am not brave and I had come upon them at the moment of a death. I was a stranger, in some manner I could be blamed. It is enough in these terrible times to put a man at risk of injury or worse. There is a passion of violence in the people, where several are gathered the spirit of murder is never far.

"I meant no harm," I said. "I am only a poor priest." This last certainly was an unnecessary saying, they could see what I was from my habit and my tonsure. "There is no one with me," I said.

"A priest abroad on foot, a priest hiding among the trees," another of them said, he of the white robe, and he laughed like a sob. "He has been giving sermons to the little folk." This was a young man, no more than twenty by his looks, with hair of wheat color, very ill-kempt. His eyes were pale and unsteady and set wide in his face, and there was a full color of blood in his lips. He had tears on his cheeks also.

"I meant no harm," I said again.

"Put away the knife, Stephen," the man who was the leader said to the dark man. "Do you take a hammer to a beetle?" This scornful reference to my status as priest and dignity as man was wounding to me in my helpless state but I was still too afraid to reply. Stephen returned the knife to his belt with a flourish and bared his teeth at me as he did so and it seemed to me that he did this so as to seem less obedient. I saw now that he had no thumb on his right hand.

The piebald nag had ambled forward to the edge of the clearing and lowered its head to crop at the thin grass. The cart had a cover of oiled canvas but I could now see over the wooden flap at the back of it. It was heaped with a strange mixture of things, bundles of colored stuff, robes and costumes, a gilt crown, the shape of a tree cut out and painted, also a serpent in coils and a devil's fork and a flaxen wig and a ladder. There were pots and pans there also and a brazier and tripod and a round metal tray a yard at least across.

One needed not to be so well versed as I in Ockham's Law to find the minimum explanation for such diversity of effects: they were traveling players and they were wearing scraps of costume against the cold.

My fear lifted, no one fears players, but I felt the situation to be difficult. Having stumbled on a death I could not simply walk away. I began talking, which is my usual resource. I am copious in speech when I find a theme and my time disputing in the schools has sharpened this fluency and taught me the figures of rhetoric. I explained to them that it had been the spirit of inquiry that kept me there watching and I went on to point out that this is no vice as the vulgar sometimes suppose, calling it curiosity; on the contrary the spirit of inquiry in a well-ordered soul springs from a sense of common humanity, and I quoted in support of this that saying of Publius Terentius Afer, *"humani nil a me alienum."*

There are times when we are blind to the ill-matching of things. I stood prating among them, with the dead man lying in our midst staring up at a sky that was darkening with snow. I would have gone on longer, warming to my theme, but I was interrupted by a snorting sound from the man called Stephen, and the boy clapped his hands. I was offended by this disrespect but then bethought me of the figure I must cut, with my threadbare cassock and rag-haired pate. I had been on the road since May and the hair had grown; I had tried to restore the tonsure with the razor I carry in my pack but made a botch of it, having to work by touch alone.

"Well, he can talk," the woman said. This was a slattern with hair falling into her eyes, young still but with hardship like a mask on the face of her youth. Such faces we see often among the people now, not true faces but masked by sufferings. She wore over shoulders and chest a piece of stuff checked in red and white squares, the Fool's shoulder cloth taken from the cart, with a hole in the middle, through which she had passed her head. "Creeping about in the bushes, what did he hope to see?" And she raised the muddy hems of her skirts some inches and spread her knees and the gesture was slight but very lewd, a whore's gesture. Then the fair-haired staring one, who to me had the look of disordered nerves, made a mime of crouching and peering, gulping all the while with lecherous eagerness in his white angel's smock and it was very well done but no one spoke or laughed. They were in grief for the dead man, they had loved him. I was of no account to them because I had come through the trees like a thief, they knew me for a fugitive, outside the limits of my diocese without permission. Traveling players are wanderers also, but these had a badge of livery, they had the license of a lord.

The one I knew for the leader knelt again by the body and drew the eyelids down and turned the face aside, very gently, with the flat of his hand against the cheek, so as to bring the flaccid lips together again, over the bloodless gums. "Alas, poor man, poor Brendan," he said. He looked briefly up at me. "You came at a bad time," he said in a tone without animosity. "You came with his death. You will favor us now by going on your way." But I did not move because with his words an idea had come to me. "We shall have to put Brendan back on the cart," he said, looking again toward the dead face.

"On the cart? To what end? Where should we take him?" This came brusquely from the man called Stephen. I saw the master-player swallow and some red of anger came to his face, but he did not speak immediately. "Take yourself off while you still can walk," Stephen said violently to me—the anger was in him also.

"Wait," I said. "Let me travel with you. I am not big but I am strong enough, I could help with the scaffolding and the boards when you put up a booth. I write a good hand, I could copy parts and prompt the players."

Yes, the proposal came from me, the first idea, but I had

no thought in the beginning of taking part in their plays, of practicing their shameful trade, *artem illam ignominiosam,* forbidden to us by Holy Church. My only thought was to travel with them and this because of the badges the leader wore, which meant that the company belonged to a lord and had the lord's letter of license and would not be set in the stocks or whipped for vagabonds as happens to those accounted fugitives or masterless men and this has also befallen men in Holy Orders who have no warrant from their bishop. Also present to my mind was the wronged husband: if he came after me I would find safety in numbers. But I swear it was never in my thought to take the dead man's place. Had I but known the toils of evil this wayside death would lead us into, I would have gone my way with no further syllable and all the haste I could summon.

As yet there had been no answer, though I heard some laughter among them. "I can hear confessions," I said. "I can expound the Scriptures. It is true I have no benefice and I am outside my diocese, but I can still perform the office. I would not ask for wages, only the food and lodging we chance on as we go."

"Of your expounding we have no need," the master-player said. "No more than of your Latin. As for putting up a booth, men will come forward if help is needed and ask nothing but a quart of ale and a ha'porth of cheese and that is less expense than an extra belly to fill all along the road."

But he was looking at me in a different way now, on his face had appeared an expression of considering. He had heard the need in my voice, fear too perhaps—a solitary man is prey to fear, unless the solitude be embraced for Christ. "A priest can usually sing," he said. "Have you a voice for singing?"

"Why, yes," I said, in some wonder—I did not see yet where he was coming to. And it was the truth, I have been commended for my voice. It is not of great strength but clear and sweet of tone. Along the way, when my money was all spent, I had used it sometimes for profane purposes; out of my need I had sung in taverns and sometimes I had been pelted, but more often fed and given space to sleep.

"Brendan was a marvel in song," he said. "He outdid the nightingale."

"He would sing like an angel," the flax-haired one said, with that strange, infirm eagerness of expression that belonged to him. "He would plant his feet and raise his head, it was as if a tree sang with its leaves."

"His song was like a rope of silk," Stephen said. His voice was deep and had a drinker's hoarseness in it.

This was the first instance I noted of a habit common with them, of speaking with one voice like a chorus, but yet in turn, so it resembled a scale in music. They had changed, they were sharing with me their knowledge of the dead man. But I could not easily think of sweet airs coming from the throat that was Brendan's now, nor of that poor crooked mouth moving with song. His face was turned to hog's lard in that cold weather. "How did he come to his end?" I asked.

"Yesterday, walking behind the cart, on a sudden he cried out and fell down," the fourth man said, speaking now for the first time. This one was older, scant-haired and long-jawed, with bright blue eyes. "He could not get up, he had to be lifted," he said.

"From that time he could not speak," the boy said. "He had to be taken on the cart."

"Sounds he could make but no words," the leader said. "He was ready of speech before and full of jokes." He glanced at me and there was a fleeting horror in this glance. I saw that for him the dumbness that had befallen Brendan, singer and joker, was a thing of nightmare. "Sing something, you," he bade me.

I should not have obeyed because he had something in

mind for me not admissible and I suspected it by now. Playing on a public stage is forbidden to us by Council, first at
Exeter and then at Chester, also by edict of our Father in
Christ Boniface the Eighth, and so I knew I was placing
myself in danger of degradation. But I was hungry and sick
at heart.

"Do you want a love song," I said, "or a song of good
works?"

"A love song, a love song," Stephen said. "The devil take
good works." He said this without smiling. In all the time I
was with them I only once saw him smile.

"Good works he will not take, brother, but he will take
the rash of speech," the old one said. The dog sat close to
him and listened to his every word. He clapped his hands at
me. "Come, sing," he said.

So I gave them "Lenten Is Come with Love to Town,"
singing alone in the clearing, unaccompanied at first, then
the boy played the melody along with me on a reed pipe
that he took from somewhere about him.

At the end of it the leader of them nodded his head. Then
he turned and went to the cart and found there two rag balls
such as jugglers use, one red, one white, and he called me to
catch and flung the red one, speaking and throwing at the
same moment almost, and I caught it in my right hand and
he threw the white one to the other side, high this time and
a little wide so I had to take two steps and this second ball
also I caught and held. Someone behind blocked my left heel
while I was still off-balance and I stumbled but I did not
fall.

He nodded once again and said to the others, not looking
at me, "He is quick enough and neat in movement and he
sees well to both sides and steps clean. The voice is good
enough. He will not be another Brendan, but with teaching
he might do."

This praise, though far from fulsome, gave me pleasure

and that is to my shame. But there was something in him, some power of spirit, that made me want to please him. Perhaps, it occurs to me now, it was no more than the intensity of his wish. Men are distinguished by the power of their wanting. What this one wanted became his province and his meal, he governed it and fed on it from the first moment of desire. Besides, with the perversity of our nature, being tested had made me more desire to succeed, though knowing the enterprise to be sinful.

He looked at them now and smiled a little, a smile that made his face young. "We took Margaret because Stephen wanted her, and a stray dog for Tobias. Why not a runaway priest who may be of use to us all?"

He was the leader but he needed still to persuade them. As I was to learn, everything touching their life as players was debated among them on equal terms.

"He will be known by the tonsure," Stephen said. The woman was with him, she was not for them all as I had first thought. I knew it by the way she kept close and listened to his words. But she had eyes for me too, mocking but not altogether so, and I resolved there and then that if taken into the company I would not return these looks, so avoiding sin. Besides, Stephen was dangerous. "He will be known for a runaway," he said now, turning his dark face from one to another of them.

"Yes," the one in the white robe said, "he is traveling without license or he would not seek to join us. He can be held in any parish, and then they would close down our play."

"A hat, let him wear a hat," the old one said. He had been seeming to take no notice of the talk, pushing at the dog in play, much to the brute's delight. "His thatch will grow soon enough," he said. "Not like mine." He grinned to reveal a paucity of teeth and passed a hand over his scant gray hair and weathered scalp. "He is a likely man for a player, priest or no," he said. "He wants to be of our company, so much is written on his face. And we are in need of a sixth, now that poor Brendan is gone."

"In sore need, that is the heart of the matter," the leader said. "We have practiced the Play of Adam and we begin with that as all have agreed, and we cannot do it without six, and three parts doubling. This man came upon us at the bidding of a thought, as do the Virtues and Vices that contend in a Morality. He came as Brendan died and we will do best to profit from it. That is my word as master-player of this company by our Lord's order. And so will we do, with your consent, good people."

There was silence among them for a short while, then each in turn nodded as the leader looked at him. The woman he did not look at. When all had signified assent he turned back to me and asked me my name and I gave it, Nicholas Barber, and he gave me his, Martin Bell, and he told me how the others were named. The fair-haired one was known only as Straw, and they called the boy Springer, though whether these were their true names I do not know. The old one was Tobias. The woman said her name was Margaret Cornwall.

So with a song and a game of catch that children might play I was elected a member of this company of goliards, and so I accepted the election. Had I refused, had I left them in the clearing there, the dead Brendan in the midst with all his sins upon him, I might have now been a sub-deacon again, with all privileges restored, back among my books in the Cathedral library. However that may be, the terrors that come to me still at night I would without doubt have been spared.

Two

I T IS THE WEAKNESS of my case that I can only seek
pardon by revealing the pass I had come to. But this in
turn was the result of my own folly and sin. And so I seek
indulgence for a fault by revealing faults anterior to it. And
there are further faults anterior to those. It is a series to
which I see no end, it goes back to my mother's womb.

First there was the shame, to cause distress to my Bishop,
who had given me the tonsure, who had always treated me
like a father, because this was not the first time I had left
without permission but the third, and always in the May-
time of the year at the stirring of the blood and this time the
reason was different but the stirring was the same, I had
been sent to act as secretary to Sir Robert de Brian, a noble
knight and generous in his benefactions but not of discern-
ing taste in letters and in short a very vile poet who set me to
transcribing his voluminous verses and as fast as I copied
them he would bring others. All this I endured. But then in
addition he set me the task of transcribing Pilato's long-

winded version of Homer. It was the month of May, the birds were singing with full throats, the hawthorn was breaking into flower. I made up my pack and walked out of his house. It was December when I met the players, the flowers of spring were long withered. Misfortunes had come to me. I had lost the holy relic that I had kept for several years and bought from a clerk newly come from Rome, a piece of the sail of St. Peter's boat. I lost it at dice. And then, that same morning that I met them, I had lost my good cloak, leaving it behind in my coward's haste. I was chilled to the bone when I came upon them and hungry, and discouraged by these blows of fate. I wanted to be in community again, no longer alone. The community of the players offered shelter to me, though they were poor and half-starved themselves. This was my true reason. The badge of livery was only an argument I used for myself.

To make my transformation complete I had to wear Brendan's stained and malodorous jerkin and tunic and he had to be dressed in my clerical habit, there being no alternative to this exchange except the outlandish scraps of costume on the cart. It was the woman who undressed Brendan and put my habit on him. The others would not do it, nor would they watch it done, though men for whom travesty was common enough. But I watched, and she was deft and tender with him and there was kindness in her face.

When it was finished Brendan lay in his priest's garb, a man who in life had been impious and full of profane jest. And there stood I in the garb of a dead player. But now an argument sprang up among us. Martin was for taking the dead man with us on the cart. "Brendan died unshriven," he said. "We must bury him in hallowed ground."

"The horse is slow enough as it is," Stephen said. "The roads are bad and there is snow coming. We have lost time already, with the broken wheel. We are sent to Durham for Christmas to play there before our lady's cousin. We cannot fail in it and still keep favor. The first day of Christmas is eight days from this one. By my reckoning we are still five days' journey from Durham. Shall we travel with a dead man for five days?"

"The priest will ask for money," Straw said. He looked round at our faces with that strange, febrile eagerness of expression. As I was to learn, he never stayed long in one state of mind but was led always by some vein of fancy all his own, gloomy and exuberant by turns. "We can bury him in the forest," he said. "Here in the dark wood. Brendan will sleep well here."

"The dead sleep well enough anywhere," Margaret said. She looked at me and there was provocation in her look but no malice. "Our priestling can say the words over him," she said.

"Margaret has no voice in this," Martin said. "She is not of the company." He said these words directly to Stephen, whose woman she was, and I heard—and surely the others did also—the tremor in his voice of feeling barely held in check. His right hand was clenched and the knuckles had whitened. "You would leave him here?" he said. For me, who did not know him then, this passion was strangely sudden and strong, as if not only his plan for Brendan was being questioned but with it some cherished vision of the world.

No one answered at once, such was the fierceness in him. I think Stephen was making to answer but Martin spoke again, in a voice that had deepened. "He was like all of us," he said. "While he lived he never sat at his own hearth or ate at his own table. Pot and jar he needs no longer, but he will have a home properly made in the earth for him, deep enough, and a roof over his head at last."

"Brendan had his habits, he would not have denied it himself, and too much ale was one of them," Tobias said.

"But drunk or sober he played the Devil's Fool better than anyone you ever saw."

"To make his grave what would you use?" There was contempt now in Martin's voice. "Adam's spade and Eve's rake that are made of wire and lath-wood? The ground is hard with the frosts of these last days. We will labor till dark to make a grave and it will not be deep enough to keep the crows from picking his eyes."

"We have knives," Stephen said.

He had meant for digging but there was now a terrible pause while Martin looked steadily at him and he returned the look. Then the boy Springer stepped forward before either man could say more. He was always a peacemaker, though the youngest, one of the blessed who will be known for the Children of God. "Brendan taught me to tumble and stilt and play the woman," he said. "We will not leave him in a ditch, for our hope in Christ, good people all." And to amuse us he gathered the trailing pieces of his shawl round his shoulders and made gestures of a woman who is vain of her long hair.

"Do you remember how he would caper round on those shanks of his?" Tobias said. "He would step short as if he could not help but fall."

"He never fell save by intention," Martin said. He had recovered from that passion of feeling, now that he felt the others turning to his will. And he spoke directly to me, including me in these memories of Brendan, and I was grateful, there was a sweetness in his nature that made him attentive to others when not disturbed in feeling or crossed. "He would wear the cap and bells with ass's ears and a half mask," he said. "Or sometimes a mask with four horns like a Jew's."

The one they called Straw laughed suddenly, a sobbing laugh, and struck his knees with open hands. "He would steal the Devil's ale and spill it in his lap, being in such haste to drink it," he said. "You would see him shuffle with his knees kept close and the ale dripping down while the Devil hunted high and low for his can."

"You would just think he had pissed himself," Springer said tenderly.

"Do you mind how he would comfort the Devil with his song?" Stephen said. It was to Martin that he spoke and I saw it was the way his pride had found of making peace. "He made his own songs," he said. "He made the words himself. When the Devil was sad because Eve would not take the apple at first, Brendan sang a song of his own to lighten the Devil's mood. 'Were the World All Mine,' that was the song."

Springer took up his reed pipe and played the air and all joined in the song for a verse, singing together there and looking at one another's faces as they sang, in the cold weather among the bare trees.

> "If the world belonged to me
> I would make a broad way
> From the hills to the sea
> For Fools to ride . . ."

Thus they mourned Brendan with his own song and were again in harmony one with another. I see them again now, their faces as they sang, that gleam of light touching the dead oak leaves, Straw's white angel robe, the round copper tray in the back of the cart. But what chiefly lives in my mind is the strangeness of our nature, that men should come close to violent quarrel over the disposing of one poor husk of flesh in a time of plague and blood like ours, when every day is a feast day for Death, when we have seen the dead piled in the streets without distinction, rotting in carts, heaped together in common pits for graves. That is some years past but there is again an outbreak in the north here, a stronger strain, even winter does not halt it. The fields lie untilled, many die of famine, they fall and in haste they are shoveled away in obscure corners. Bands of brigands infest the countryside, peasants in flight from their dues of labor, soldiers returning from these endless wars with France, men who have known nothing but murder from earliest life. In parishes you will find less than half the folk left alive. And few will know clearly where those they love have been laid. Yet there was this care over one poor player.

Little more was said of him either then or later. They had sung his epitaph. Nor was there any further argument about taking him on the cart. Then and there he was lifted up. He was laid down among the masks and costumes with a coil of rope for his pillow, and covered with pieces of scarlet cloth that they carried to make a curtain at the back of the stage. After this we set off again on our way. And so I began my life as a player.

Three

I N THE DAYS THAT FOLLOWED Brendan stayed on the cart and we placed over him boards and sack cloth to keep him from rats in the yards of the poor wayside inns where we stayed, sleeping sometimes on straw in the outbuildings of the yards, sometimes all together on pallets in the wretched rooms of hovels that claimed to be inns. Martin paid all scores from the common purse. He kept the money belt always on him and his dagger within reach. The purse was thin and there was the cost of Brendan's burial to think of. None of the players had money left except for Tobias, who was thrifty; the others had spent their share of the division. In these days we passed through no place peopled enough to make a performance worthwhile, villages were reduced to hamlets by pillage and plague, houses stood empty and half-ruined, dust of rubble was thick in the streets. The snow held off but the weather was cold, keeping Brendan's body from corruption.

During all this time Martin was tireless in teaching me.

He spoke to me as we went along. All walked usually behind the cart, taking it in turn to lead the horse. He told me
of the qualities a player needs, quick wits, easy movement, a
ready tongue for parts that are not fully written. He showed
me the thirty hand movements that all must learn and made
me practice them, reproving me always for my clumsiness,
the stiffness of my wrists and shoulders. Making these signs
must be as natural and easy as any normal habitual motion
of the limbs or the head. Over and over again he made me
do them until my movements were fluent enough and the
angle of the hands and position of the fingers as they should
be. He was as relentless in this schooling as in all else. The
slightest praise from him had to be earned doubly over. He
was proud of his art and passionate in its defense—everything with him was passionate. His father before him had
been a player and had brought him up to it.

No opportunity for my instruction was let pass. In the
intervals of our traveling he would put me to practice, when
we paused at midday to eat our scraps of cheese and rye
bread and pig's blood sausage and drink our thin ale, in the
poor lodgings we found at night, and in spite of all weariness—Martin shed weariness in the eagerness of his teaching. He gave me the Play of Adam to con over, the pages
tattered and the hand poor—I vowed to make a fair copy
when time allowed it.

All of them helped me, each in his different way. And
each, in doing so, revealed something of himself to me.
Straw was a natural mime and very gifted in it. He could be
man or woman, young or old, without the need for any
speech. He had been traveling alone until seen by Martin at
a fair and taken into the company. He was a strange excitable fellow, very changeable in his mood, with bouts of
staring gloom. Once during these days he fell and writhed
his body on the ground and Springer held him and wiped
his mouth till he came to himself again. He did three times

for me the mime of one who finds he has been robbed, showing me the importance of head movement and clear gesture and the frozen moment of the mime when all the meaning is expressed in stillness.

Springer gave his age as fifteen but he was not sure of it. He did women's parts. He could sing high and his face was like rubber; he could pull it any way and twist his neck like a goose, so that you laughed to see it however many times it was done. He was sweet in nature and fearful and without malice. He and Straw were close and kept much together. He came from a family of jongleurs—his father had been an acrobat who had abandoned him when he was still a child. He showed me cartwheels and somersaults at the roadside as we went. He could arch his back like a hoop, with only heels and head touching the ground and from this position spring forward like a whip and come upright. This I could not hope to emulate but tumbling I practiced when I could. I am nimble and light of foot and achieved some skill in it, with Straw and Tobias holding a rope at the height I had to clear.

It did not seem to me that Stephen had such skill in playing as these two. He was not so concerned in it as they. But he was tall and deep-voiced and had a memory for his lines. He did parts requiring dignity and state, God the Father, King Herod in rage, the Archangel Michael. He had been an archer for some years, in the pay of the Sandville family, Earls of Nottingham—the same that owned this company of players. He had raided for them and fought for them first against Sir Richard Damory and after against the Earl of March. He was captured in a skirmish by the Earl of March's men and they severed his right thumb at the first joint, disabling him for ever as a bowman and forcing him to change trade. This had been done at the lord's behest; nevertheless Stephen was an admirer of the aristocracy and proud of his part in these bloody disorders. "I know men who had their eyes put out," he said. "I was lucky." He carried a bronze medallion of St. Sebastian, patron saint of archers, in a pouch at his belt. It was a great mark of friendship on his part when on the third day he showed this medallion to me, also his mutilated thumb.

Margaret was with us for his sake. They quarreled, though less in these days, I was told, as they had not money enough to get drunk on. She had played the whore in her time and made no great secret of it. She was harsh-tongued and gentle-handed. She had no part in the playing and very little in the counsels we took among us. She earned her place by washing and mending for all and cooking when there was something for the pot. This last often depended on the sixth man, Tobias, who played Mankind and doubled the small parts and did attendant demons. He also could play the drum and the bagpipes. He took always a practical view of things and was listened to on account of this. He was our handyman, seeing to the horse, keeping the cart in repair as best he could, making wire snares for rabbits and bringing down a quail or a partridge sometimes with his sling. He was patiently trying to teach the dog to flush out game birds but so far without any success, the brute was full of goodwill but brainless. Tobias taught me how to fall without doing hurt to myself. He never spoke about the past.

The Devil's Fool, which part I had taken over from Brendan, should by tradition be a juggler too, but this I could not hope to learn in the time. What I could do I did, and practiced hard to improve whenever there was opportunity, so as not to be a cause of disappointment to them, and in particular to Martin, who had been the most concerned in taking me and besides I was drawn to him. There was a tenderness of feeling in him. And he was constant, though with a constancy yoked always to his own will and purposes. I treasured his rare words of praise and uttered them again to myself as I walked with the cart or had my turn, the road being level, to ride for a while with Brendan, and sometimes also in the night when I lay awake. I set my heart on succeeding as a player.

I learned from them that Robert Sandville, their patron lord, was away in France fighting for the King. They belonged to him and were bound to perform when required in the hall of his castle and at those times they received wages. But of late this had been rarely. Most of the year they were obliged to travel. They had Sandville's warrant but he gave them no money while they were outside his lands. Now, with her lord away, the lady had sent them as a Christmas gift to perform for her cousin in Durham, Sir William Percy. They were hoping for generous treatment there. "If we live so long," Stephen said darkly. We were footsore, progress was slow in the hilly country north of York.

Then once again Brendan decided our destiny. He had begun to smell foul the day before. Traveling on the cart with him one noticed it more, the jolting of the cart moved his body under its covering of red cloth and with these stirrings of movement the smell of his dissolution came dank and unmistakable on the chill air. It grew stronger by the hour and we had no oil or essence we could use to cloak it. There was a fear that before we could reach Durham his corruption would be shed on to the costumes and curtain pieces that were needed for the play. Martin called a meeting to discuss the matter and we sat there at the edge of the road. It was raw weather with a thickening of mist in the air and our spirits were low.

"It is bad luck to be bearing the stink of death," Straw said. He looked gloomily at the heap below which Brendan lay. "It will ruin our play," he said. He was easily downcast and had a great fear of failing, more than the others.

"It will not be easy to wash out," Margaret said. "Some of the costumes cannot be washed by any means. How would you wash the suit of Antichrist, that is made of horse's hair?"

"It stinks enough already without help from Brendan," Springer said. It was this garment that he had been wearing as a shawl against the cold. "It stinks of vomit," he said. And he got up and walked away from us in an ill-humor very uncommon with him.

"Before ever we get there," Tobias said, "before ever we get to Durham it will be a cause of offense in the places where we stay."

"If you had listened to me," Stephen said, "we would not be facing such a difficult thing. It is not too late even now. We need take him no farther. Let us leave Brendan here to leak into the ground, as he will do soon or late for all our pains."

"The question of what to do with Brendan was settled when we talked before," Martin said. "That he has now begun to stink can make no difference. We must have him buried sooner, that is all."

This was said with Martin's customary firmness but it solved nothing, and we were sitting there in silence when Springer returned. "There is a town," he said. "Down there below us, not so very far." And he gestured across to the other side of the road.

We looked where he pointed but saw nothing. "It is on the other side," he said. In a body we went across. We followed Springer up a short slope of rising ground, grass-land, cropped close by sheep. From the crest of this, looking westward, we saw a broad valley, well wooded, with a straight river flowing through it and on the far side of this the roofs of a town, wreathed in woodsmoke, with the tower and keep of a castle on a height beyond, the lower part veiled in mist but we saw the battlements and pennants flying. And it seemed to me that some errant light touched these roofs and also the turrets of the castle, like the light that had come when they sang over Brendan. There was a reflection, perhaps of armor, from somewhere high on the walls. We gazed for a time without speaking, at the shine of water through the bare willows, the shrouded houses beyond. And as we looked there came a sound of bells, very faint, like shudders in the air.

There was a guidance in it, as there had been in my first coming upon them. What is accident to the ignorant the wise see as design. Springer had flung away from us in a petulance rare with him. He had followed an impulse to leave the road, climb the slope . . . The town was there, the castle was there, the bells were sounding. None of us so much as knew the name of the place. A gift of fortune then. But gifts can also be intended for our harm. I leave the judgment to those who read my words to the end, whether this gift of the town was for harm or good.

There and then we decided. We would turn aside to the town, see Brendan buried there, and perform the Play of Adam so as to replenish our purse. Martin kept count of the days and by his reckoning it was the Feast of St. Lazarus so there would be folk at leisure. And we would have time enough still to reach Durham for the day promised.

The town was some three miles distant on a road that descended by gentle degrees. When we drew near we stopped and came off the road in order to prepare for our entry into the town. We gave the horse oats and water and freed him from the shafts for a while so as to rest him for his hard labor now to come: he would have more than Brendan to draw through the streets of the town.

The costumes we dressed in did not belong together in one play but were chosen for spectacle only. In the middle of the cart a space was cleared and here stood tall Stephen as God the Father in a long white robe, with a gilt mask covering all his face and a triple crown on his head like the Pope's, made of paper stiffened with glue and stained red. With him was Martin dressed as the Serpent before the Curse, still inhabiting Eden, with feathered wings and a smiling sun mask.

The rest of us walked alongside or behind; Springer in a Virgin's gown, girdled at the waist, and a wig dyed yellow with saffron; Straw as a man of fashion in a white half mask, a surcoat with trailing sleeves and a pointed hood; Tobias as Mankind, barefaced, in plain tunic and cap. As for me, they gave me the horsehair suit of Antichrist to wear and a devil's horned mask, and armed me with a wooden trident that I was to jab with as we went along, at the same time jibbering and hissing. It was my first role.

We put Brendan in the rear of the cart with our clothes heaped over him and the copper thunder tray laid on top. We hung the cart with the red curtains and put red rosettes behind the horse's ears. Margaret led him, steady and slow so as not to overbalance God and the Serpent. She too was dressed in finery, in a frayed blue gown with slashed sleeves, her hair combed and pinned up. As we began to come into the town we made of our progress a drama of sound as well as sight, demons and angels contended with music. Springer played his reed pipe and the Serpent a viol while Mankind beat time on a drum and God marked the intervals with a tambourine. In order to drown these heavenly sounds I had been hung about with a cooking pan and an iron ladle, with which I made a great din, and Straw carried a stick with which he belabored the sheet of copper below which Brendan lay, making rolls of thunder. At intervals, when harmony and discord were in full conflict and the issue in doubt, God raised his right hand, palm outward and fingers slightly curled in the gesture of silencing, and with this the din of the demons instantly ceased.

Thus alternating between order and chaos, with the
skinny horse lifting its head to the music and stepping lively
as perhaps by habit it had learned to do, and the dog, which
was tied to the cart behind, barking loudly in excitement, in
such fashion we paraded through the streets of the town till
we came to the market square and the inn alongside.

I for one was glad when we came there. The suit of hair
was hot and close on my body, the mask was made of
paper, pressed and glued together, it was thick and airless. I
did not see well through the eyeholes and my sight was
altogether closed off at the sides. I had to remember to jab
with my trident and hiss while the music was heavenly, also
to be ready with the pan and ladle when Straw sounded the
signal on the tray, also to keep one eye on God so as to fall
silent the instant he raised his hand. I was confused by the
clashing sounds and by the faces of the spectators briefly
glimpsed, some staring, some laughing, some openmouthed
with a shouting that was not separate from the great noise
we were making ourselves. It was now that it came to me—
a lesson that was to be learned over again in the days that
followed—that the player is always trapped in his own play
but he must never allow the spectators to suspect this, they
must always think that he is free. Thus the great art of the
player is not in showing but concealing.

Adding to my disorder of mind was the sense that my
mask and the ancient, mangy horsehair suit were redolent
already of Brendan's decay. It came to me that perhaps my
mask and suit had lain next to him and I wondered if this
same suspicion was in the minds of the others. His odor we
were obliged to hide, as we had hidden his body. We
brought Death into the town, so much is certain. Death
rode with us on the cart, he was there in the midst of our
panoply and fanfares while we wooed the staring folk for
their custom. Certain too that Death waited for us there, for

he can be here and there together at the same time. By God's grace I came out from the town again, Death waits for me still. But time has done nothing to dim the memory of it, the clamor of our entry into the town, the close mask and evil-smelling suit of Antichrist. And the fear of dissolution.

Four

FOR FIVE PENCE we hired a barn, with a cowshed adjoining, in the inn yard, where we could keep our things and also sleep. Five pence was a good deal for such a lodging but the innkeeper would not take less. "Why should I haggle for pence with a band of players?" he said, and he wiped his hands on his greasy apron with an air of being above such base considerations. "There are cows in the byre, or I would have asked six," he said.

This innkeeper was a low-browed, brawny fellow, with one eye turned inward. He was scornful of us and did not scruple to show it, though he would profit from our play because it would be done in the yard of the inn. But he was of those who boast where they despise, as if to justify contempt. "Others will take the barn if you do not," he said. "Why should I haggle with vagabond players when I am preparing rooms for the King's Justice, who comes here from York and is expected hourly?"

Martin said nothing to this but looked him coldly enough

in the eye. He had taken off his angel's mask but still wore
the wings. I had kept on my mask, being afraid to remove it
because of my tonsure, and through the eyeholes I saw
Springer and Straw exchange glances and Straw crossed his
eyes in imitation of the innkeeper and wiped hands on an
imaginary apron, doing it however in such a way that his
hands were crossed also, a gesture very comic in his present
dress of fashion, fortunately not observed by the innkeeper.
I wanted to ask why the Justice came here at such a time of
year, and perhaps would have done so in spite of the muffling mask, but he left us to drive away a blind man who
had come into the yard to beg. There was a little ragged girl
with him and she had pissed against the wall.

When he returned we agreed on five pence and Martin
paid it. It was a bare place with an earth floor, but it was
dry, the roof was good, and there was a stout door to it with
an iron bolt and a padlock. This last was an important
matter as we had much to fear from thieves. All the capital
of the company was in the costumes and masks and pieces
needed for setting out the playing space. These had been
added to over the years, some made, some bought, some,
for all I knew, acquired by the very means we now had to
guard against.

We changed out of costume and unloaded everything,
including Brendan, whom we carried all in a group in his
covering of curtain and laid in a corner. Here inside, among
smells of dung and straw and trampled earth, his presence
was not so evident.

The inn yard was busy with people coming and going.
There were some soldiers in breastplates talking in the middle. By the arches on the inn side of the yard there was an
old woman with a tray of buttons and two young ones with
squares of green in their sleeves to give notice they were
whores. The blind man and the little girl had returned.
There were shouts for service from guests in upper rooms

and a serving man passed along the yard to the staircase that led up to the gallery. An ostler was trying to stable a black palfrey on the other side of the yard but it was high-metaled and made nervous by the noise and bustle, it reared and shied at obstacles that only it could see, and its hooves clattered and sparked on the cobbles. Slung over the saddle was a tourney shield bearing a crest with a coiled serpent and bars of blue and silver. A squire in early middle-age, bareheaded, wearing a coat of thin mail under a brown surcoat, came forward and spoke to the horse and calmed it. He was dusty and stained with travel, and on the breast of his surcoat was a badge with bars of the same colors, blue and silver. I heard him call to the innkeeper to have wine sent up for himself and the Knight whom he served.

All this was like a public show for me. I felt no relation to anything I saw because no one knew what I was. I did not know myself. A fugitive priest is a priest still, but an untried player, what is he? I could breathe and I could see, now that the mask was off. I was set apart, in a different space, as the spectator is always. And I wondered if these people too, who seemed able to move as they wished about the yard, were in truth constrained to behave as they did and were only pretending to be free, as we ourselves had done when we came in procession through the town.

Then Martin, with Tobias as witness, went to give an account of the death and arrange matters with the priest. There were things for the rest of us to do. Brendan continued to give us labor. He could not be taken to the church in my clerical habit nor could we deliver him naked. He had to be dressed in his own clothes again—and again by Margaret, who was as gentle with him as before. The habit was hung from a rafter to freshen it as far as could be; it was now become part of our common stock. Meanwhile I wore the high tunic and sleeveless jerkin of Mankind and a

woolen cap borrowed from Stephen, which was too large
for me and came down over my eyes.

These things were scarcely done before the same ostler
came with straw and sacking for our beds. It was mid-
afternoon only, but the light was already beginning to fade.
Stephen and I were standing at the barn door. I am inquisi-
tive by nature and talking comes easily to me. I asked the
ostler about the squire and the one he served.

"They stay the night here," he said. He was young and
round-faced and had a simple look of importance at knowing something we did not. "They have ridden from Darling-
ton today, and that is a good long road," he said. "He is a
knight with a fief in the Valley of the Tees from what I heard
tell. They are either poor or mean. The squire gave me one
penny only."

"One penny is not bad reward for holding a nag's head,"
the sardonic Stephen said. "I do it hours together sometimes
without being paid at all."

But the ostler was one with small play of mind, who took
everything strictly by the letter. "There was not just the
one," he said, with the beginning of anger. "There was also
the warhorse to stable, a beast that could back and crush
you like a fly if you did not look to it."

"True, it is little," I said. "Perhaps the fief is small. Why
do they come here?"

"They will have come to take part in the jousting," he
said. "There is to be six days of jousting lasting till St.
Stephen's Day. The Lord has sent to knights from many
parts. This will be one who travels from tourney to tourney
and lives by the prize money. He has small hope of prizes
here, with Sir William taking part, that is the Lord's son and
the very flower of knighthood and has never been unhorsed."

"Which lord is that?"

"Why," he said, with a look of surprise for our ignorance

on his simple face, "that is the Lord Richard de Guise, who holds this town in his fief and the land all east from here to the sea. He is known everywhere for his giving of alms to the needy and his punishing of wrongdoers and his godly life—he would have none such as you in his Hall."

It was his castle then that we had seen from the road that morning. Into my mind the vision came again: the huddled houses in their pall of smoke, the battlements and pennants beyond, rising into light, that gleam of light on metal from among the parapets.

He was turning away when I said, for no more reason than idle curiosity, because it had been in my mind since talking to the innkeeper, "Well, what with that and the Justice that is expected you will be kept busy."

The light was failing now from moment to moment, there were brands being lit and set in their brackets along the walls of the yard, and also above in the rooms of the inn there were lights showing. The light from the brands made shifting ripples on the dark stone of the walls and moved on the damp cobbles. I could hear the breathing of the cows behind me. "Why does he come," I said. "What brings the Justice from a great place to a small in the days before Christmas?"

The ostler's face had been in shadow but as he turned away the light fell briefly on it and I saw that his expression was changed, it had become unwilling. "I do not know why," he said. "The trial has already been. I cannot stay longer, I am called for above."

"Better than to be called for below." This, with a gulp of laughter, was from Straw, who had come up behind us from inside the barn. They had lit a torch inside and his disheveled hair had a bright halo around it.

"What trial?" I said. "Has there been a crime then?"

The ostler hesitated, divided between caution and the pleasure of knowing. "God's pity, yes," he said at last.

"Thomas Wells was murdered. He was found the day before yesterday on the road outside the town. There is Roger True's daughter found guilty of it by the Sheriff and she is to be hanged." He spoke the names as if they must be familiar to all.

"The man will have betrayed her," Margaret said, as if there could only be that one reason. She too had come to join us at the door. "He will have played fast and loose with her."

"But if already she is found guilty," I said to the ostler, "what brings the Justice with his retinue here?"

He made no answer to this, but shook his head only and went quickly from us, passing through the arches and so into the inn.

"There is swift justice in this town," Straw said. "Only two days since he was found on the road and the woman is tried and condemned already."

No more was said about the matter then and I thought we would have no more to do with this murder, but I was wrong.

Martin and Tobias now returned, each in his different way affected by what they had to say to us, Tobias seeming abstracted and more interested in his dog than anything else, Martin white-faced with rage. The priest, a fat, slothful fellow with a thick tongue, he said—this a piece of scorn very typical for anyone not neat in movement and nimble of speech—this priest had demanded four shillings for burying Brendan. They had gone to seek him at the church and been told by a man cutting holly for Christmas where he lived. A young woman had come to answer.

"His leman," Tobias said.

"To be a priest's whore," Margaret said, with a toss of her head. "She was not dressed for keeping house, I daresay."

It was more than any of us had thought possible. He had

asked a shilling for the ground, twopence for the gravedigger, and two shillings and ten pence for himself.

"Two weeks' wages for a laboring man." Straw brushed a ragged sleeve over the glinting stubble on his face. "For mumbling over a hole in the earth and the lump of clay they fill it with."

"It has brought us low in the common money," Martin said. "We are left with eighteen pence and one half penny."

"You have agreed then?" Stephen said. He was one of those who must cavil and question and Martin's fury turned on him now. "Do you start carping again?" he said. In rage he was a man to beware of. He had no relief from it in gesture or shouting, which was strange, for he was accomplished in all the gestures of feigned emotion, also that emotion of players that becomes real by feigning. But passion felt directly was like a suffering he had to contain. He had no expression for it save this pain of stillness. Beyond the pain—and only a touch beyond—there was violence.

"We agreed together before ever we came here," Springer said. "Do you not remember, Stephen?"

"We did not set a limit on the price," I said, joining in debate for the first time, as I felt now to be my right. "Just as it is true that *ignorantia juris non excusit,* so also it can be said of the price, *pretium,* and this is a principle very important both in—"

"I knew we would get a ladleful of Latin before long," Stephen said, glowering at me, but I was not offended because I saw that for him this diversion had been opportune, even necessary. And it came to me then that all the members of this company were playing parts even when there was no one by but themselves. Each had lines of his own and was expected to say them. Without this no debate could be conducted, here among us or anywhere else in the wide world. The parts perhaps had been chosen once, fanatical Martin, Springer the timid and affectionate, Stephen the disputatious, Straw wavering and wild, Tobias with his proverbs and his voice of common sense; but the time of this choosing lay outside memory. Now I too had taken my part within this company. I had my lines to say. It was my role to moralize and lard my talk with Latin and turn all to abstraction, so that Straw could pinch his nose and nod wisely in mockery of me and Stephen could glare and Springer laugh and Martin's anger be muzzled. The only one without a part was Margaret, who had neither public voice before the people nor private one among us.

Martin took his eyes from Stephen slowly. "These worms that eat the common body," he said. "As ignorant of doctrine as of grace. They know only how to sleep through a confession and drink a flagon and exact their dues. And the better to do this they work with the nobles and keep folk tied to the land."

His words were insulting to the Church, but I made no protest. To say truth, since I had embraced this trade of player, I wanted to succeed in it, and a sure way to fail was to mark myself off from them. To serve the time is the mark of wisdom, as Tobias might have said; and the time had made me a man for songs, not sermons.

Besides, what he said about priests in country parishes is true in large measure—at least it is true of a great many. Many are unlettered and incapable of expounding a text. They live in open concubinage and charge the people for their services. In some parishes the priest will not perform the Eucharist without being paid beforehand in cash or kind.

As to his other charge, of aiding the lords in securing land services, I said nothing to this either, but it is the merchants and men of business in the Commons who make statutes to keep wages down and prevent men from offering their services to new employers. Men are taken and branded as fugitives, on the forehead for all to see, only for leaving their lord's land without permission. But it is not the Church that makes these laws. It is true, of course, that the Church frowns on traveling folk and works always to keep men in their place. Where sufficiency is, there is stability, and where stability is, there is religion, *ubi stabilitas ibi religio.*

As I have said, I did not argue for priests. I did not want to defend this one, who asked so much money, because we all suffered alike from his cupidity. On the other hand, they knew I was in Orders, they would register my silence, they would think me craven. "Priests vary in their nature as do other men," I said. "They are as various as players are."

Tobias spoke now, for the first time since his return. "There is good and bad in every kind," he said, "and all are needed to make up the world. Speaking of priests, there has been a murder in the town. A woman is condemned for it and it was a monk brought her to be questioned."

Martin turned to this as if he needed the change. "We heard them speaking of it in the porch of the church," he said. He spoke softly and in his eyes was a vagueness as of strong feeling past. "He is the Lord's confessor and lives there with them in the castle. He is a Benedictine."

That word comes back to me now and his look saying it, spent with his rage, and the gleam of torchlight on the straw we sat on. I could hear the moving and breathing of the cows. The smell of their dung and their pissy straw was strong in the barn and this was mingled with the dark smell of Brendan in his corner. Margaret sat with spread legs mending a rent in Adam's smock, her face turned to the light. This parting of her legs under the skirt disturbed my mind and I prayed within myself to be delivered from evil. From hooks and nails in the barn there hung our masks and curtain stuff and costumes, the Serpent's wings, the Pope's hat, the shoulder pieces of the Fool, the horsehair suit hanging from the rafter like a great bat. The barn had been made into a place of strangeness. The sheet of copper rested against one wall and the torchlight moved in eddies over it, as if the surface melted colors, blue and gold and red from Eve's wig and her glass beads that were hanging up together. My sight was troubled by these shifting colors and reflections and by the blurring fumes of the torch.

"We were talking of it to the ostler." Straw looked round, his eyes unsteady, his wild hair glinting in the light. "He did not like to talk of it," he said, "though he was ready enough to talk otherwise."

"It was a robbery," Tobias said. "They found the money in her house. The Monk found it."

"They have always a good nose for that," Stephen said.

There was no time for more talk, we had to dress ourselves and prepare to put on the Play of Adam. And I was nervous, there was a tightness in my chest, I had no mind for other thoughts. But the shadow of this crime was over us already, though I did not know it then. It is over me yet.

Five

THE TROUBLES of that day were not over. While we were preparing to put on our play a band of jongleurs came to the inn to the sound of drums and bagpipes, and began at once to set out their pitch against the wall of the yard, opposite the entrance—the best place. Martin, already in the short white smock of Adam before the Fall, emerged from the byre to find a bear tethered to the wall, rope-walkers putting down their mats, and a strong-man unloading chains from a handcart. For some moments he stood there, bare-legged in the cold, as if unable to believe his eyes. Then he moved quickly toward them. Stephen and I followed, he already in God's long robe. We were much outnumbered—there was a fire-swallower there also, busy lighting his brazier, and a family of tumblers.

Jongleurs travel in groups and entertain people wherever they can, in great halls, at tournaments and archery contests, at fairs and marketplaces. In this they resemble players, but unlike us they have no leader and there is no general meaning in what they do, they can combine together or break away.

Because there was no leader it was difficult for Martin to find someone to dispute the place with. But he settled on the tumblers, as they were a family—man and woman and two shivering shaven-headed boys. He told the man that the space was already taken, speaking at first in a tone of explanation, not roughly but with a visible effort of control. But the man began to argue and the woman broke in shrilly to support him and the strong-man, understanding what was happening, dropped his chains with great clatter on the paving stones and came toward us. This man was very big, taller than Stephen and thicker in body, though much of it was fat. He was bald and very ugly and he wore a copper ring in one ear. He snorted like a wrestler as he drew near and raised his hands as if he would take Martin in a grip. This I think was meant more in threat than in earnest, in order to inspire fear in us, but when he was still two yards off Martin took a step and launched a kick at him, turning slightly so that his foot struck the man's body heel first, and very high for a standing kick—it caught the man on the left side, just below the heart. He did not fall but leaned heavily forward and sought for breath deep within him and all could hear this searching.

How the fighting would have gone on from this I do not know. Stephen, who was a brawler by nature, had pressed forward. Martin had raised a fist and might have struck again while the advantage was with him. But then the innkeeper came with a stout serving man at his side and he said the place was ours because it had been promised, also because we had hired the cowshed in the yard and he got money from that whereas he got nothing at all from the jongleurs and knew moreover that he could not extract anything from such people because they do not charge anything for entrance but take round a hat, which we also did when there was no enclosure of the space, but here in the yard there was a way to come in.

The rope-walkers began taking up their mats again, the tumblers talked sullenly among themselves. The strong-man backed away to his cart, cursing us and promising revenge. The innkeeper, seeing his advantage, now demanded from us a quarter of the takings for the use of the yard and for having defended our rights.

The blood had drained from Martin's face, though whether this was because of the dispute with the jongleurs or the innkeeper's demands I could not determine—he was passionate about money as he was passionate about all things. I expected he would speak in protest but strong feeling had for the moment disabled him, as it does with some natures, and he remained white-faced and silent.

The others had come up now and each was affected in his own way. Springer, already in the costume of Eve, his eyes round with fear below the flaxen wig, sought to distract us from quarrel by strutting and preening. Straw was speechless, I think by sympathetic closeness to Martin—he had a nature like a loadstone for feelings of others, they gathered within him and the casing of his body was too thin for them. He was staring now and clutching himself in agitation and this was strange to see, dressed as he was in the robe and wings of the Serpent before the Fall. Tobias, who knew Martin better than any, put an arm round his shoulder and spoke quietly to him. It was left to Margaret to bargain with the innkeeper. She said he should not get anything more because he had not asked for it before, when we had agreed together for the barn and the use of the yard. He replied, with the reasonable air of one who deems himself well in the right, that he had not known then that the space would be disputed.

At this I could not forbear breaking in. This cheating innkeeper was also a fool in logic, a fault I find hard to overlook. "It is in the nature of all contracts that the parties to it should have a mutual sense of *posse* as well as *esse*," I told him. "A promise provisional on circumstances, when these are not stated, is not a promise at all, but mere blandishment and deceit. There could be no faith in any bond if all behaved as you do."

For only reply he called me a prating fool. In the end he agreed to twopence in every shilling. He said he would set one of his people to stand at the entrance to the yard to keep away the drunken and any that were known to be troublemakers, but his real reason was to keep watch on the money that was taken. This thief of an innkeeper, had he been the one at Bethlehem, would have taken every groat from Joseph and Mary even for that poor stable where Christ had his nativity. Judas, they say, was born that same night . . .

We had lost time over this and had to make haste—people were already coming in. My fear of failure had been growing as the time approached. With the dark we had set torches against the wall so that the people would see us edged by light, beings of flame. This was Martin's idea. For the moment only two of the torches, those in the middle, had been lit. The Fatal Tree was against the wall, with a paper apple stuck on a twig. We had the barn for a changing room, which meant that we would have to pass through the people.

When all was ready, Adam came through the people to speak the Prologue. He came and stood with the two lighted brands directly behind him. He had on a black cloak over his smock. Waiting in the barn, we heard his clear voice:

"I pray you give your ears and eyes.
See Eden lost by Satan's lies . . ."

I looked round the barn door and watched him standing there with the light behind him. There was some talk and laughter from the people, not much. They had not come in great numbers; a glance was enough to show that; the yard was less than half-full. I was dressed for the first of my roles, that of an attendant demon, in a horned mask and a red, belted tunic with a rope tail attached, at the end of which was an iron spike. I carried with me a devil's trident for roasting the damned. I had nothing to say for this first part, I had merely to attend to Satan and make forays among the people, hissing and jabbing with my fork so as to create alarm. This I thought of as fortunate, as it accustomed me to being in public view before my more important role of Devil's Fool.

When Martin had said his lines he moved quickly away from the light, made his way to the far corner of the space, and lay down there. Covered by the dark cloak, with his face hidden, he seemed to disappear. This too had been his idea, he had thought of it when first we saw the way the brands were set against the wall. In all concerning spectacle he was clever and quick beyond any of the others.

Now it was time for Stephen to appear as God the Father and make his slow majestic way through the people. In order to increase the impact of his presence he walked on six-inch stilts, tied to his legs below the robe. The gait of a stilt-walker has a sway of majesty about it, something stiff and slightly hindered, as God might move among men, and quarrelsome Stephen looked truly like the King of Heaven with his gilded mask and triple crown, as he paced from light to dark and back again, delivering his monologue.

> "I, God, great in majesty
> In whom no first or last can be
> But ever was and aye shall be
> Heaven and earth is made through me
> At my bidding now be light . . ."

On this, Tobias, in his first role of an attendant angel, in wig and half mask and wings briefly borrowed from the Serpent, came through the people with a flame and lit all the brands along the wall and so made a flood of light over everything. God walked now in the light of his creation and the dark heap of Adam was visible in the corner.

> "Now man we make to our likeness
> With breath and body him to bless
> Over all beasts great and less
> For to hold sway . . ."

Adam crept out from under his cloak, rubbing his eyes, his naked legs shapely, though pimpled with cold. And now Straw appeared as the Serpent before the Curse, in wings hastily recovered from Tobias and a round and smiling sun mask. He came through the people and he was singing as he came, a crooning chant that women sing at the spinning wheel. Adam was lulled to sleep by this song, but not very quickly. He kept catching himself up with a start every time the Serpent paused in his singing and the Serpent grew impatient at this and turned to the people to make the sign of impatience, which is done by raising the hands to shoulder height with the fingers pressed back and turning the head stiffly from side to side.

While the people were watching this lulling of Adam, Eve came quietly along the side of the yard with a dark shawl over her head. When Adam finally slept God swayed forward on his stilts and raised his right hand and turned it quickly at the wrist in the sign of conjuring, and at this Eve dropped her shawl and stepped in her yellow wig and white smock into the brighter space, and was born. She was barelegged also. She caused laughter and lewdness among the people by her vanity and preening and by the sway of her boy's buttocks as she walked before Adam when God was not looking. When God retired to rest there was a game of catch between them, he clumsily reaching for her, she evading.

Now came the time for me to follow Satan, played by Tobias in the red robe that also served for Herod and a very hideous red and yellow mask with four horns. I hissed and jabbed and made sorties among the people and flipped up my spiked tail behind. I put much energy into this performance and some effect it had—several of those watching hissed back at me, a child started to cry loudly and the child's mother shouted words of abuse. This I took for success, my first as a player. But it came to me again that the people were not so many, and I knew this thought would also be in the minds of the others.

I had to get quickly back to the barn and change into the mask and motley of the Devil's Fool and take the tambourine, because Satan retires to Hell and sulks when Eve refuses at first to take the fruit and he has to be comforted. There was hostility toward me from the people. A man tried to pull off my demon's mask as I went by but I avoided him. Despite the cold of the evening, I was sweating.

There was only God inside the barn, sitting on the straw, drinking ale. He seemed depressed and did not speak to me. It took little more than a minute to strip off my demon's dress and put on the Fool's tunic and shoulder pieces and the cap and bells. But it was long enough for me to become aware again of Brendan's presence under his heap of straw in the corner. My mask now was a plain white one, full face, with a long nosepiece like the beak of a bird. I shook my bells and struck the tambourine as I went back through the people. I was a different person now, they did not hate me. They knew me for a japer, not a demon. I understood then, as I passed through the people and shook my bells and saw them smile, what all players come to know very well,

how quickly shifting are our loves and hates, how they depend on mocks and disguises. With a horned mask and a
wooden trident I was their fear of hellfire. Two minutes
later, still the same timorous creature as before, with a
fool's cap and a white mask, I was their hope of laughter.

I was discovering also the danger of disguise for the
player. A mask confers the terror of freedom, it is very easy
to forget who you are. I felt it now, this slipping of the soul,
and I was confused because in body I was the more re-
stricted—the mask did not admit much light to my eyes and
I could see nothing at all to the sides. Close before me,
through my narrow slits, I saw the ornate and fearsome
mask of Satan and I heard the strangely remote and hol-
lowed voice of Tobias bemoaning his failure and loss.

> "Ghostly paradise I was in
> But thence I fell through my sin.
> Earthly paradise by God's gift
> Man and Woman dwell within.
> I have tried all in vain
> By my wiles to bring them pain . . ."

I had learned Brendan's song and now I sang it and I
shook the tambourine in time to the song and sang as
sweetly as I was able, to soothe the Devil. I quavered at first,
through fear, and this caused some laughter. But my voice
strengthened as I went on and the fear fell away. When fear
dies, daring is born. I finished the song but instead of saying
the lines I had learned I made the three-fingered sign to
Tobias to show I would speak my own words.

> "If the world belonged to thee
> Lord of all things wouldst thou be
> Lord of life . . ."

It was the Fool tempting the Devil with the World, a reversal of roles. Something new. Tobias answered with words of his own also, having had some moments to think.

> "If the world belonged to me
> Women all would ready be
> To harken to the Devil."

Saying this, he made the two-handed gesture of copulation. By some instinct, instead of remaining still I began to circle round him, speaking now the lines I had learned, trying to remember the movements of hands and body that I had been taught. Tobias, though he had not known I would behave thus, made a comic business of it, craning round his horned mask to follow the tinkle of my bells, looking always the wrong way, always startled by the new direction of my voice. There was laughter at this and I joined in this laughter at the Devil and pointed and then tripped and fell, as I had been taught to do, but jarred my left elbow a little, and the laughter grew and it was sweet to me, I will not deny it. Turning into the light I was dazzled and for some moments I could see nothing and the laughter sounded in my ears . . .

Six

THIS MY FIRST APPEARANCE as a player I felt to have been a success. But afterward, with the others, I did not like to show elation because their mood was gloomy. Margaret had been set to watch the gate and take the money. She had taken one shilling and eleven pence and of this the innkeeper had taken threepence and three farthings. The hire of the barn was five pence. Our triumphant entry into the town had been too much for the cart: one wheel was buckled and would need repairing. This was beyond the skill of Tobias and he thought the cost of repair would be threepence at the least. We would be left with less than a shilling to add to the common stock. And there were seven of us and a horse. And we were promised for Christmas at Durham.

It was a clear night and very cold. A cladding of frost lay already on the cobblestones of the yard. It had a shine like satin where the light fell. Martin gave out twopence to each of us. Springer got out the brazier and made a fire with wood we had brought with us on the cart. Straw sat near it, huddled under a blanket. Tobias had still kept Satan's robe on and sat with the dog across his lap. Nobody mentioned Brendan. When they got the money Stephen and Margaret went off together.

There was some talk among us about the play. Straw, whose esteem of himself was always low, took the poor attendance as a failure of his, and sought to shift the blame. Hugging his knees unhappily, he gave as his opinion that God had been too long-winded and Satan too smooth. "There was not enough movement in it," he said. "People cannot listen for so long."

"They can listen if there is something to listen to," Tobias said. He was angered by the reflection on his playing. "You want all to be done in gesture," he said, "but it is words and mime together that make a play. It was not our fault to-night, it was the jongleurs that took away our custom."

"Eve can be played without words," Springer said. He had come to sit beside Straw and they shared the blanket. "I have done it so," he said.

"Eve, yes," Martin said. "Adam also. They are not personages, they are a man and a woman. But God and the Devil need words." In the torchlight his face looked famished and gaunt. The high bones of his cheeks and his narrow eyes gave him the look of a wolf and this impression was strengthened by the way he leaned forward and raised his shoulders against the cold. I was struck by his loneliness and his severity—two things inseparably mixed in him. The burden of our failure lay on him; yet he was intent to correct us, to make his meaning plain. "God and the Devil are personages," he said. "God is a judge, Satan is an advocate. Judging and pleading need different ways of speech. In that difference is the true play, if someone could be found to write the true words."

"Well, certainly, there is reason in that," said Straw,

whose view of things was formed by his feelings of the moment and changed direction as rapidly as did these.

Springer's eyes were beginning to close as he felt the first heat of the fire. Weariness smoothed his thin face. "What can words do?" he said. "God and the Devil both know how the story ends." He spoke slowly, like a sleepy child. "And the people know it too," he said.

"They know how the story ends," Martin repeated, also speaking slowly, in what might have seemed mockery at first, but his eyes were fixed and on to his face had come a half-startled expression, as if at some recognition.

He was about to say more but I did not wait, I had been distressed to hear him speak of our Father in Heaven as a circumscribed being, the more so as I follow William of Occam, the Great Franciscan, in believing that God dwells beyond the reach of our reason, in absolute liberty and power. "No words can bring us to the nature of God," I said. "Our language is human, it is we who made the rules of it. It is the sin of pride to think that our human language can lead to knowledge of the Creator. And to speak of the person of God as you have done is to break the Seventh Commandment."

That strange quickening look had gone from his face now. He was looking at me with pity for my understanding. "We are talking of *plays,* brother," he said. "It was the Church that first made God a player. The priests played Him before the altar and do so still, as they also play Christ and His Holy Mother and others, to help our understanding. As a player He can have His own voice, but He cannot take the voices of others. The Father of Lies has more privilege, who can borrow the tongue of the Serpent."

"It is damnable to speak of God in such a way, as if He were no more than a voice among other voices."

Seeing my distress, he smiled but not to deride me. His smile was lazy, coming slowly, at odds with the tenseness of his face in repose. "In some way we have to see Him, if we put Him in a play," he said. "Let us see Him then as a great nobleman, owner of very vast estates. Adam and Eve are His tenants, in bondage of service. They do not pay their dues of obedience, they want to possess their holding. If He grants them all they ask there will be nothing to punish and then what is left of His power?"

This was worse still and I began to get to my feet, but he smiled again and raised his right hand in God's gesture of silence and said, "You did well tonight, Nicholas, considering that it was the first time. You fell badly at the end, but urging Satan with his own words was a bold thing to conceive and you made the signs clearly and stepped neatly round him. All of us felt this."

At these words I forgot the argument and felt my heart swell with pleasure. More to me than the praise itself was the proof that he had watched me carefully, noted what I did. Martin made himself loved, even in his profanities. And profane he did not feel himself to be, not when he talked of playing. For him the life of the play was set apart from the life outside it, with its own rules of behavior and speech, to which all were subject, strong and weak, high and low. I did not see the danger of it then, God forgive me my folly.

Silence fell upon us now as we relaxed in the warmth from the fire. I thought of our Play of Adam and of that Garden lost by our first parents at Satan's prompting. Unlike most, I know where it lies. In the library of Lincoln Cathedral, where I had held my office of sub-deacon, there is a map which shows the place of it, at the farthest limit on the eastern side, quite cut off from the rest of the world by a great mountain. God keeps it still and walks there sometimes in the evening. Meanwhile it waits empty for the Saints to repossess it. I thought how strange it was that such a garden should stand empty and how delightful to be among that company of the Blessed, to walk amid dwellings of jasper and crystal, through groves where every kind of tree and flower grows and birds sing with unwearied throats, where there are a thousand scents that never fade and streams flow over jeweled rocks and sands that shine brighter than silver. Cold never comes there nor wind nor rain. There is no sorrow or sickness or decay. Death himself cannot pass over that high mountain. And all this we had figured in an inn yard with a tree cut out of board and a paper apple painted red and for a brief while people had taken it for Paradise. I have heard it said that the mountain beyond which it lies is so high that it touches the sphere of the moon, but this is difficult to believe as it would cause an eclipse . . .

I was near to sleeping when Martin got up and came over to me and asked me to walk with him, speaking quietly, not including the others. I rose at once.

"I cannot sit still or keep in one place after the playing," he said as we crossed the inn yard. "I am too stretched in my mind over it, not in the body so much, but the mind draws the body with it. It is not work like laboring, to make the limbs heavy and bring sleep, unless one is like poor Springer, who has fears but no nerves and is only fifteen and still growing. It is worse tonight because of the money."

For a while we walked through the streets of the town. There were not many folk abroad now. The mud was hardening with frost. It was a black night with no stars visible— that earlier clearness of the sky was quite gone. We carried a lantern on a stick and this swinging light was all we had to see by. I could smell snow on the air and feel the massing of snow clouds in the dark, making the night thicker. We came to a small tavern, a single mean room with benches and rush mats on a floor of beaten earth. The light was poor and the smoke stung our eyes but there was a fire burning and places near it.

We drank thin ale and ate salt fish—all the place could

offer. Martin was silent at first, staring into the fire. When
he spoke it was again about playing and he kept his voice
low so as not to be overheard—he guarded all to do with his
trade very jealously. "My father was a player," he said. "He
died of the plague when I was the age Springer has now.
When we played in the towns the folk came in numbers to
see us. Now a few jugglers and a dancing bear can take half
the people away. We are only six. For our playing in Durham before the cousin of our lady we can do the Play of
Adam and the Play of Christ's Nativity, since these we have
practiced. With time for preparing we can also do the Play
of Noah, the Rage of Herod, and the Dream of Pilate's
Wife."

He looked up somberly and met my eye. "We are only
six," he said again. "What can six do? All we own goes on
the back of a cart. Now there is coming more and more the
big cycles of plays that are put on by the guilds. From Scot-
land to Cornwall it is happening, wherever people live together in numbers. In Wakefield now, or in York, they will
put on twenty plays, they will go from the Fall of Lucifer to
Judgment Day and they will take a week to do it. They have
all the wealth of the guild to call on and they do not count
the cost as it serves the fair name of their town. How can we
match them?"

His eyes had widened. He spoke feelingly but there was a
look of vagueness on his face as if the words he was saying
were not the true source of his feeling. "We cannot match
them," he said. "In Coventry I have seen Christ resurrected
from the tomb with block and wheels and hoisted up to
Heaven, where clouds were hanging from cords not visible
to the eye. I have seen a beheading of the Baptist where the
player was changed for an effigy by the use of lights and
trapdoors and so cleverly was it done that the people noticed nothing and they shrieked to see a headless corpse. I
knew it then, when I heard them shriek at a bundle of straw

dripping with ox blood. The day is over for poor players who travel with the Mysteries. We have worked and done our best and we are skilled and we sit here and drink stale beer. Between here and Durham we shall have little more than acorn meal to swallow, with our own snot for a sauce, unless Tobias can wire a rabbit, which in this frozen weather is not easy. No, brother, we must find another way. The others look to me, I am the master-player."

He looked at me and nodded heavily, but there was a brightness now in his look. "Springer spoke good reason, even though he slept as he spoke," he said. "The story of the Fall is an old one, the people know how it ends. But supposing the story were new?"

"A new story of our parents in Paradise?"

"This murder you were talking of," he said, "we heard something of it on our way to see the priest."

I am gifted with foreknowledge, as I began this account by saying. Sometimes we do not know we are waiting until the awaited thing arrives. It arrived now with these words of his, which should have come as a surprise but did not. The first dread, I felt it then, in that poor place, seeing the light on his face, light of temerity. "The ostler at the inn spoke of it," I said. "I did not think you had taken notice of this talking."

"Why, yes," he said. "It is our trade to take notice of such things. These were all women. They had voices long drawn-out, as women have when they agree together about a bad thing and find pleasure in so agreeing." He opened his eyes wide and turned down the corners of his mouth and in a voice little louder than a murmur he imitated this talk of the women: "Ye-e-es, she was always so seemly, who would have thought such a thing of her, eyes for men she had not . . . Well, neighbors, what man would want her for a wife?" He stopped and looked seriously at me. "All the voices were the same," he said. "Like a chorus. Why would no one want her?"

"When she had done such a thing—"

"No," he said, "they were speaking of the time before the murder. Perhaps she is ugly, perhaps she is a witch."

I did not want to speak of it but his will was stronger, eclipsing mine—then and later. His desire, the light of interest on his face, compelled me. I fed this interest with the scraps he had given me himself. "It was the Lord's confessor found the money," I said. "He found it in her house."

"Not her house," he said, "her father's. She is a young woman, unmarried. She has no house."

"How do you know this?" I asked him, and watched him shrug slightly. There was a strong smell of the privy out in the yard. The night soil gatherers had not yet passed this way. I was weary now and fearful, though I did not know of what. I had a sudden memory of the ostler's face as he turned from shadow into light.

"I spoke to the priest's woman while I was waiting," Martin said. "Tobias stayed outside because with him he had that cur he loves so."

"You asked her . . . ?"

"Some few questions, yes."

I waited for a moment but he said nothing more. Even then I could not leave the matter. "All the same," I said, "it is strange, it is unusual, that a woman without help would kill a man in that fashion."

"What fashion? We do not know how the killing was done."

"I mean on the open road. A woman might kill a man in rage or jealousy, choosing a time when he was off his guard."

"It was not a man, it was a boy of twelve years."

I found no answer to this. Thomas Wells was a child then. Small puzzles removed do not make a lessening of wicked-

ness. A woman could more easily kill a child, yes . . . He
had questioned the priest's woman more than a little, I saw.

He smiled now and began to speak in signs to me, something he did often, and always without warning, for the
sake of giving me practice. He made the snake-sign of tonsure and belly for the monk; then the swift chopping motions of roof and walls; then the sign of urgent question,
thumb and first two fingers of the left hand joined together
and the hand moved rapidly back and forth below the chin
—a sign very like the one that signifies eating except that in
this latter case the thumb is uppermost with the elbow held
out and the movements somewhat slower.

How did the Monk come to be in the house?

He waited, pressing back his head to show the need for
an answer. I am sorry to say it but truth compels me, I
craned forward my head to show eagerness and did my best
to make the rapid tongue movements of lechery, though
could not do it with the gibbering speed I had observed in
Straw.

Martin laughed at this. He seemed in great good humor
now. "But she did not look at men," he said, "if we are to
believe the good dames." And he compressed his lips and
made a gesture of the right hand against his cheek to sign
blushes, then with both hands the motion of drawing close
a shawl, like Chastity in the Morality Play.

It was all we said on the matter that night. And because in
the end he had laughed and made a joke of it, my fear was
overlaid. The wildness I had sensed in him, the readiness to
transgress, these I found passing reasons for. He was disap-
pointed at the poor custom for our play, he was unhappy at
our poverty. Thus I sought to reassure myself. I did not
properly know him yet, did not know that everything with
him was serious. Perhaps that was why he chose to walk
with me that night, one not so familiar with his nature, so

that he could talk without betraying his intention. I am sure now that the intention was already there in him.

I know this from what more I know of Martin now; at the time it was beyond my suspecting. But the foreboding was there. With memory aiding, it is not so difficult to relate events as they follow in sequence. But the dread that comes to natures like mine, that is not so easy to trace, it moves in lurches, forward and back, it catches at new things. That fear I felt in the tavern at the power of human desire, a power for harm or good, I feel it still. The nature of power is always the same, though the masks it wears are various. The masks of the powerless are various also. I remember what was said between us that night and the changing expressions on that lean face of his. He had done already what he could always do with frightening ease: he had passed from notion to intention to strategy as if between them there were no curtain, nor even a screen of mist.

Seven

WE ALL ATTENDED Brendan's funeral, even the dog —kept close by Tobias on a piece of chewed rope. I had thought at first to stay behind, because of the need we would be under to uncover our heads and I was still with the ragged tonsure of my other life. Margaret it was who found the solution—simple enough, though none of us had thought of it, being still fixed on the idea that I should wear some form of head covering at all times. "We will shave him," she said, in the flat tones she always used, keeping her mouth half-closed so that the words came out in a mutter without changing the lines of her face. Margaret had suffered much hardship and degradation of body and was unwilling now to offer the world anything superfluous. In spite of this she had a very deft and gentle touch, which I knew before by the way she handled poor Brendan. With Stephen's razor and water from the pump in the yard I was shorn without a scratch.

"And if anyone asks why, we will say it is because of the

ringworm," Springer said. Being a fearful and pacific soul he always thought of reasons and excuses. And he knew it was a good answer because he had suffered this affliction himself as a child, and had his head shaved by a barber.

The church was on a hillside and from the graveyard we could see across the wooded valley where the river ran, to the bare uplands beyond, which had a faint sea light on them—the land tilted down from there to the sea. This was a country of low hills and wide valleys. The trees were bare now, save for the stubborn russet of the oaks. The slopes of bracken beyond the river were the color of rust. All was still —the day was windless. The sky overhead was dark, gravid with snow.

Brendan's last costume was a pauper's shroud. There was no coffin. We watched him lowered into the earth by Martin and Stephen to wait there for the Last Days, that cannot now be long in coming. Our hope and prayer for Brendan was the same as for ourselves, that though his mortal body was lost in corruption he would be dressed again in glory when the graves give forth their dead.

The frost that had come with night had loosed from the tips of the grass blades now and they showed a darker green. There was a tide mark of death in this graveyard, a mounded line where the victims of that summer's plague were buried in their common pit. The Black Death has returned to these northern parts after a fallow time of a dozen years. Death is never sated. Now once again in every graveyard we see this tide slowly gaining on the green. Over against the wall of the apse the priest's four sheep were grazing where the grass had grown in shelter and so escaped the frost. Beyond the plague mound there was a single new grave, very small, a child's grave, with a tarred wooden cross. Beyond it, above the trees of the valley, I saw a heron rise on heavy wings.

The priest pronounced the final blessing in a hasty nasal

and as he did so it began to snow, large soft flakes that paused in the still air and sidled, as if cautious how to fall, unwilling to gash themselves. At the first touch of the snow, the priest began to make his way back to the church with unseemly haste. He had taken his money already in the vestry. So there was nothing now to do, as the snow thickened, but to see the first spadefuls thrown over Brendan and then set out back toward the inn.

But Martin did not come with us at once. He lingered behind and I saw him go and speak to the gravedigger. As we passed along the path that led round the graveyard to the church gate, I fell back and left the others and crossed the frosted turf and the line of the plague pit and came to the small grave. The earth was freshly dug. There was no name on the cross; there would scarce have been time to cut the letters. When had the ostler said he was found? The day before yesterday, in the morning. Swift justice in this town, as Straw had said. Swift disposing of the victim also. But perhaps after all this was the grave of some other . . . I stood for some moments gazing while the snow darkened the earth of the grave, and as I did so I fell into a state of mind familiar to students, at once attentive and vague, as when faced with some faulty or imperfect text. Often it is when one waits without question that the truth of the author's intention comes drifting into the mind. Hesitant, circumspect, like this first snow.

I was in this state still when I rejoined the others. We waited for Martin at the lych-gate, sheltering under the roof of the gateway. I was standing a little apart, just under the roof, at the roadside. For no particular reason I moved forward a little and looked down the road toward the town. The snow made a mist and at one moment there was nothing but this mist and at the next there were dark shapes in it, advancing slowly up the hill, two riders and with them a great black beast whose head rose high as theirs and it had red eyes and above its head there moved with it a shape of red, dark red in the white of snow, and I knew this for the flame of the Beast's breath and I knew what Beast it was and what manner of riders these were and I crossed myself and groaned aloud in my fear, seeing that the Beast had come and my soul was unprepared.

Hearing my groans the others came round me and they also looked but what they said or if they spoke at all I do not know to this day, I saw only that Springer fell to his knees, then Stephen, a moment later. My own legs were trembling but I did not fall, I wrestled as best I could with this agony of fear because Christ said that he who overcometh shall not suffer a second death, he shall come into the New Jerusalem. And I knew also that the witnesses in Revelation that were slain by the Beast from the Pit later ascended into Heaven. But they had kept faith and I had not.

They came on at a steady pace and all my courage was spent to keep them before my eyes and pray to be delivered from evil. But with the Pater Noster still on my lips I saw that the floating shape of red was over the head of the first rider and kept constantly above him as he moved, it was a tent or canopy of some sort. And then I heard the voice of Tobias saying that it was a knight and squire with a warhorse and I saw Stephen scramble to his feet and offer to help Springer up, as if his only purpose from the first had been to perform this service.

Tobias's words were true. What I had thought the eyes were red patches to block the animal's sight at the sides. And after some moments more I saw that there was a long tourney lance slung along its flank and projecting before and behind. Over the head of the leading horseman there was a cover of some red stuff, perhaps silk, wetted now, very thin—the dull light came through it and fell on the pale face of the rider. The horse he rode was a black stallion, which lifted its head and snorted at the touch of the snow. The one behind kept his head lowered and the long plume of his hat came over his brow but as they drew nearer I knew him for the squire who had helped stable the horse— this same restive palfrey—at the inn the night before. He was riding a gray mare and leading the charger on a short rope, this last a huge beast, the one the ostler had complained of, also black. The shield lay on the saddlebow and I saw again the crest with coiled serpent and bars of blue and silver. But the truly strange thing about the Knight was this square of silk above his head, which I had taken for the breath of flame and which had frightened me so that my heart knocked still against my ribs. It seemed of his own devising, resting on canes attached to the girth trappings of the horse, two before and two behind, and at its forward edge hanging down in a fringe, protecting him in large measure from the snow that came against his face. The silk was darkened with wet and it cast a reddish shade and within this the Knight sat upright on his horse, richly dressed as for a visit—he wore a red velvet bonnet and a sleeveless red surcoat of the kind that is fashionable now, open at the front to show his high-necked white tunic. He was young and his face was calm below the finery of his hat and a long scar ran down the left side of his face from below the temple to the line of the jaw. His gaze swept over us briefly and calmly as he passed by, and we lowered our heads. Then they were past, going on at the same steady pace up the hill. I went out into the roadway and looked after them and the snow lay cold on my eyes. There was smoke rising from somewhere above. It seemed to me that I could make out the battlements of the castle keep but with the snow and the smoke it was not possible to be sure. Knight and squire merged with the haze of smoke and snow, vanished from my sight.

Men respond to fear in different ways. I tried to hide

mine by talking. "They will be going up to the castle," I said. "There is to be ten days of jousting, so I heard at the inn. It will last until St. Stephen's Day. I have never seen a knight ride under cover in that way."

"Nor I," Tobias said, and he spat to the roadway. "He was afraid that the snow would spoil his bonnet. All their life is in show and gear."

Straw uttered that strange laugh of his, that sounded always like a sob. "And ours is not?" he said. "They are like us, they are traveling players." He had been frightened too, I knew it from his laughing air of relief. "All they need they carry with them, just as we do," he said.

Of us all, Springer was the only one who admitted to having been afraid, perhaps because with him fear was always such a close companion. "I thought for a while it was Antichrist coming," he said. "I had rather be a player and make people laugh than go from place to place knocking other folk out of their saddles." With slight movements of the shoulders and right arm, eyes fixed and eyebrows timorously raised, he mimed a fearful knight at a joust. This was funny because he was also miming his own fear and ours, and everyone laughed except Stephen, who had been as frightened as any but sought to disguise this now by voicing displeasure at our disrespect.

"They know how to fight," he said. As a former bowman he had seen knights in battle, which we had not. And he was always a great defender of the nobility, I think through a naturally worshipful attitude toward the rich and powerful —perhaps this was why, it occurred to me now, on his stilts and with face gilded, Stephen was so convincing in the part of God the Father. "Half a hundredweight of plate armor," he said, looking with dark disfavor at Springer. "On a hot day it is like having your head in an oven. They will fight on horseback from dawn to dusk in any weather God sends. I have seen them wounded in half a dozen places, blinded by blood, striking out still. You, Springer, you could not so much as lift a knight's sword, let alone strike with it."

"If they couldn't see who they were striking at it would have been better to go home," Straw said. "Flailing about like that they would be as much a danger to their own people as to the enemy. And in fact they are a danger to everyone." He was a shifting, veering fellow in his thoughts and feelings, and easily swayed; but he was always constant in Springer's defense. "Why in the world should Springer want to lift a sword?" he said now. "I am surprised you praise knights so much when it was one of them that had your thumb chopped off."

This reference to his mutilation was offensive to Stephen and might have led to a quarrel, but Martin returned at this moment and we set off together down the hill, our heads lowered against the snow. At the inn a mood of extravagance seemed to come to Martin. We had a thick stew of peas and mutton and dough puddings. We had butter to eat with our bread, and good ale. The dog feasted also, on bread soaked in the broth, and Tobias gave him a mutton bone. The reckoning for this came to eleven pence, which left us with little indeed.

Stephen and Tobias were beginning to load the cart but Martin halted them. "There is a matter to discuss," he said. "Let us make a fire—there is wood enough still."

We set the brazier at the door and left the door open and sat inside in a half circle, looking toward the fire and the inn yard beyond. The snow fell steadily, muffling the cobbles with white. Flakes drifted through the doorway and hissed on the fire. We were well fed and comfortable for the moment, on the straw there, looking at the bright flames. There was a steam of drying clothes about us and there was the smell of straw and cow dung and the sharp stink of the horse.

He began by telling us what we knew well enough already: the takings had been poor, we had very little money left, and we were still some days' journey from Durham, where the lady's cousin was expecting us for the Christmas entertainment of his guests. How many days' journey it was not possible to say: this snow would make the roads more than ever difficult. "And we have scarce the pence for two days' feeding," he said—he kept returning to our poverty.

"Why then did we spend so freely on the mutton?" Springer asked, a childish question because he had known the cost full well before but been greedy for the meat. Now, with his belly full, he was reproachful.

"We must keep in good heart," Martin said. It is my belief that he spent the money on purpose so as to restrict our scope for choosing. He leaned forward now and reached his palms toward the fire, and this looked strangely as if he were gathering for a spring. Once again I was aware of something wolflike in him. But only the sinful and devious heart of man could have given his face the look it wore now, haunted with his idea, calculating still the best way to broach it with us. "There is a way for us that I have thought of," he said. "It is something we can do that the jongleurs cannot. But we must stay in this town some time longer in order to do it."

"Why do you go beating about?" Stephen's dark face was blank for a moment, then I saw his brows draw together. "What is it you have in mind for us?" he said.

Martin glanced round at us once more, but briefly. His expression was calm now, and grave. "Good people," he said, "we must play the murder."

These words brought a silence to the world, or so at least it seemed to me. There was no sound among us, our bodies were still. Outside in the yard the clatter of hoofs and the sound of voices were hushed also—or I became for the moment deaf to them. When silence falls on the world there is always one small sound that grows louder. I could hear the whispering and sighing of the snow and this sound was within me and without.

It was Tobias who brought the sounds back again; they came with his voice. "Play the murder?" he said. On his face was an expression of bewilderment. "What do you mean? Do you mean the murder of the boy? Who plays things that are done in the world?"

"It was finished when it was done," Straw said. He paused for a moment or two, glancing round into the corners of the barn with his prominent and excitable eyes. "It is madness," he said. "How can men play a thing that is only done once? Where are the words for it?" And he raised both hands and fluttered his fingers in the gesture of chaos.

"The woman who did it is still living," Margaret said. "If she is still living, she is in the part herself, it is hers, no one else can have it."

I had never heard Margaret speak before in any matter concerning the playing, but Martin did not reprove her; he was too intent on the argument. "Why should it make a difference?" he said. "Cain killed Abel, that was a murder, it is something that happened and it only happened once. But we can play it, we play it often, we play also the manner of its doing, we put a cracked pitcher inside Abel's smock to make the smash of his bones. Why cannot we play this town's murder, since we find ourselves here?"

Tobias was shaking his head. "There is no authority for it," he said. "It is not written anywhere. Cain and Abel are in the Bible."

"Tobias is right," I said. I could not keep silent though it meant going against him. What he proposed was impious and I felt fear at it. In this I sensed a difference from the others. They were astounded because the idea was new but they were not troubled in soul, except perhaps for Tobias—though this would come later to all. "In Holy Writ there is sanction," I said. "The story of Cain and Abel is completed by the wisdom of God, it is not only a murder, it has its continuing in the judgment. It is encompassed within the will of the Creator."

"So is this one, and so are all the murders of the world," Springer said, and his thin face—face of the eternal orphan —already had the light on it of Martin's idea.

"True," I said, "but in this one there is no common acceptance, God has not given us this story to use, He has not revealed to us the meaning of it. So it has no meaning, it is only a death. Players are like other men, they must use God's meanings, they cannot make meanings of their own, that is heresy, it is the source of all our woes, it is the reason our first parents were cast out."

But already, looking round at their faces, I knew that my argument would fail. They were in some fear perhaps, but it was not fear of offending God, it was fear of the freedom Martin was holding out, the license to play anything in the world. Such license brings power . . . Yes, he offered us the world, he played Lucifer to us there in the cramped space of the barn. But the closer prize he did not need to offer, it was already there in all our minds: the people would flock to see their murder played. And they would pay. In the end it was our destitution that won the day for him. That and the habit of mind of players, who think of their parts and how best to do them, and listen to the words of the master-player, but do not often think of the meaning as a whole. Had these done so, they would have seen what I, more accustomed to conclusions, saw and trembled at: if we make our own meanings, God will oblige us to answer our own questions, He will leave us in the void without the comfort of His Word.

"It has no meaning but a death," I said again, though knowing that the argument was lost. "There has not been time enough for God's meaning to be known."

"Men can give meanings to things," Tobias said. "That is

no sin, because our meanings are only for the time, they can be changed."

Yes, it was Tobias, the shrewd and equable, the player of Mankind, who was the first to speak in Martin's favor, though he had been at first opposed. The others followed.

"God cannot wish us to starve while we wait for Him to give us the meaning," poor Springer said—he was well acquainted with hunger.

"We will die by the roadside before we come to God's meaning," Straw said. He made the sign of the Reaper, a long sweeping gesture from right to left with the palm of the hand held upward. "Death does not wait for meanings," he said. "Sword or rope or plague, it is all one to him."

Stephen leaned forward and the flame of the fire lit up his darkly frowning face. "It is not so much the meaning," he said. "There is a child, a woman, a monk . . ." He paused, struggling to find words. "It is only one thing," he said at last. "It is particular. There are no Figures in it."

"It can be made a type for all," Martin said. "Can you not see it? We all have played the Morality, when we call the one who strays from the path Everyman or Mankind or the King of Life. And the Virtues and the Vices battle for his soul. So we make him a Figure for all. But it is the same battle in each separate soul, in ours and in that of the woman who robbed Thomas Wells and killed him. It is a very old form of play and the one that will endure longest."

He was using the argument of particular to general, which is admissible in logic but never in moral discourse. However, what he said about the form was true. For a thousand years, ever since the Psychomachia of Prudentius, there has been this story of the Battle for the Soul.

"We can do it as a Morality Play," he said.

Springer blew on his fingers, I think more from habit than anything, we were not so cold there near the fire. "But we have no words for it," he said. "There are some speeches of the angels and demons that might serve, but I do not remember them well, I could not do it without prompting."

"Nor I," Straw said. "And there will be little time for learning."

"We can do it in dumb-show and say lines as we think them, it need not be verse," Martin said. "We have done such things before. It will be no more than a half hour of playing, perhaps not so much." He spoke confidently now, sensing the battle won. "After it we will do the Nativity," he said. "The two will go excellently well together, a child killed for avarice, a child born to redeem our sins. Think of the money we will take, good people, only think of that. We will fill the yard."

He was looking to us for agreement. No one gainsaid him, not even I, but I cast down my eyes because I knew this enterprise was ungodly. We would be usurping the bodies of living people, our profit would come from the shedding of a child's blood.

"We will call it the Play of Thomas Wells," Martin said. There was a pause, then he spoke again but in a voice quite changed. "Come," he said, "warm yourself, good soul."

I looked up to see to whom he was speaking. In the air that quivered above the brazier the snowflakes rippled and blurred. They seemed not to fall but to waver in this trembling air and make a shimmering screen. And in this shimmer, as if the flakes clung together and clotted there, was a white moonface, smiling openmouthed. I saw the mouth work loosely, as if the words had to be chewed before they were soft enough to utter. A ragged hood came close round his face. His sparse beard was wet and the wet gleamed on his eyelashes. I had seen this idiot face before but could not remember where. He had come to squat near our fire.

"He would say something to us," Tobias said. "What is it, friend?"

There was again that working of the mouth but words

came from him now, soft and slurred but clear enough, the words of the boy's name. "Thomas Wells," he said, and peered at us with bright eyes over the glowing embers of the fire. "Thomas Wells, him they found." When he said this, I thought he might be a demon and it seemed to me that I could make out the shape of horns under his hood. The breath caught in my throat and I said some words, but cannot remember what. Springer started back. "God protect us all," he said and he crossed himself.

"It is a beggar who comes sometimes to the inn yard," Margaret said in her usual flat, muttering tone. "I have seen him also in the street outside," she said. "Good soul, what is it?"

"Him they found before the angels found him," he said. "Early in the morning they brought him home. Robert Moore's son and the youngest one of Simon the smith and the boy who herded the sheep, John Goody, them the angels found first."

"What do you mean?" Martin said. "Were there others? Who found him? Who found Thomas Wells?"

"Jack Flint found him." The idiot's eyes shone brightly. His mouth was a pool of spittal. "Sins are like stones," he said. "But children are light enough, they can fly. With these eyes I saw them." He raised a hand, palm outward, fingers splayed, and held it for a moment before his smiling face, as if shielding his eyes from rays too strong to bear and yet wishing at the same time to peer through the gaps at some sight not to be missed. "I saw over the houses," he said. "They were singing as they carried them away. The light hurt my eyes. I told Jane Goody, your child is with the angels in Heaven, but she took no comfort in that saying. She went looking for him high and low."

"Poor soul, you are touched," Tobias said, and he got up to give the man some of the bread that was left, but the

movement was too sudden, the man shifted back on his
haunches and then rose. In the space of a moment he was
gone, there was only the heated air rippling above the fire
and the falling flakes and the sound of shovels striking
against the cobbles as they cleared the snow from the yard.

"Well, he is gone," Martin said. "This Flint, who he says
came upon the boy . . . We must find out what we can. If
we are to do this thing we must know all the circumstances
of it. We must go severally about the town and talk to the
people, but as strangers, without seeming to have any purpose in it."

"They will know us for players," Straw said.

"No, they will not, most of us were masked and they saw
us by torchlight, which changes the look of a face." This
was Stephen, and to his face there had come something of
the same radiance I had seen on Springer's. Martin's idea
spread among us like a shedding of light.

"We will go about the town and learn what we can," he
said now. "When we hear the bells for Vespers, straight-
away we will come back here. Everyone will say to the
others what he has learned about the matter and we will
plan the play and decide on the parts. Then we will make a
procession on foot, by torchlight, each in his part, and we
will shout to the people what we are intending to do. Afterward we will practice the play so that we know our parts in
it, as far as time allows. Tomorrow is the day of the market,
the town will be full."

This he must have found out already, before he had our
consent. "What did you talk to the gravedigger about?" I
said. It was a question that came out quickly, before I was
decided to ask it.

"What?" For a moment he looked disconcerted, as if I
had found him out in some wrong.

"This morning, when you stayed behind."

"I asked him if he had seen the boy's body, but he said he had not because he could not see through a wooden box, and so I asked him who had made it and he said there were three carpenters in the town, it would be one of them. I asked him also if he knew who had paid to have the work done but he said he did not."

"So this idea was in your mind already?"

He looked at me steadily. "It has been in my mind for years now that we can make plays from stories that happen in our lives. I believe this is the way that plays will be made in the times to come."

I took this at the time for a true answer but not fully an honest one, thinking that between truth and honesty there lay the hope of a replenished purse. He looked away from me now and spoke to the others. "So then, we are all agreed?"

There was silence among us for some time. Then, one by one, beginning with Tobias, we signified assent. I too, at the last. The boldness of it took me. I saw fear and exhilaration on the faces round me. We were staking all on one throw. And then there was the light that came from him, we were all bathed in it. I think now it was pride of mind that led him, a worse thing than love of money. From pride there can only come brands for the burning. The resin of the wicked branch makes it flame more brightly and it may seem for a time to light up the dark; but it is soon consumed away, leaving the world darker than before. Nevertheless, having spoken against it, I gave my assent. This company of players was shelter to me, I did not want to be cast out. And then there was Martin's face and voice. He did not convince us, he infected us with his feeling. Like an infection of light there among us . . .

I spoke no more in argument against him—it was useless in any case. It may be that he was right in what he said about the nature of plays and playing in times to come. He was of those who can look forward without wavering and he had no grudge against a time when he would be in the world no longer and because of this his sight was clear. And all estates of man perhaps will change with time. That they can so change we see from the Order of the Benedictines, who do not keep to the rule of their Founder but travel abroad like this one that had found the stolen purse and was the Lord's confessor and lived with them there in the castle. We see it also in the Order of Knighthood. As we sat there round the fire, with the decision made, I thought again of the Knight, how he came riding slowly up the hill through the falling snow with the red breath of the Beast above him. I that took front rider for Death, but I know now that it was his own death that he bore about him. I remembered his pale face, the calm, reckless glance, the long scar down his cheek, that effeminate square of silk to guard his finery against the touch of the snow. The knights are a killing class, they are trained from childhood in the use of weapons and the doling out of grievous hurt. But if we believe our fathers, or their fathers before, this training had a purpose once, just as the practice of players has a purpose. As it is the purpose of the Devil's Fool to console the Devil, and that gives him license for buffoonery, so it was a knight's purpose to protect the weak against the oppression of power and to fight for Christ in the Holy Land, and this it was that gave him license to deal in death and the right to hold estates. But perhaps our fathers' fathers say only what they heard from their fathers before them and it was never true that the knights had this role, it was the Church that said it in hope to soften their ways or the king that said it to explain the grants of land he made them. They were necessary and so some role had to be assigned to them. However it may be, if they had a part to play once they have lost it now, even in battle—it is the common people who win battles, the archers and the pikemen, as these our times have abundantly shown, while the knights and their warhorses flounder in blood and are butchered together. And so they turn to sport. They deck themselves out to kill in play, as this one was decked out.

Eight

WE FOLLOWED Martin's plan. I spent my time among the stalls round the market cross and in a tavern nearby. The snow had stopped but the clouds were still swollen with it. I tried as cleverly as I could to provoke gossip, striving always to conceal from them that I was a stranger in the town. Martin had been wrong in this; to betray ignorance made people fall silent or turn away, as the ostler had done. There was something, some fear or distrust, that held them back from talking. Such a thing happened when I asked a man selling eggs whether the woman who was condemned had confessed to the crime. He looked at me for a moment half smiling, as if I had made some familiar jest. Then his face closed and he looked sullenly away.

However, some things I discovered, the most important of which was that the woman had been seen near the road on the evening that the boy was killed—it was believed that he had been killed in the evening or sometime during the night. She had been seen quite close to where he was found, by that same Benedictine, the one who had next morning gone to the house and found the stolen money there.

I told this to the others when we assembled again in the barn. Already the dark was coming. We sat as before round the fire, but it was a poor fire now, we had to husband the fuel that remained, having no money for more—we had spent almost all on this night's hiring of the barn.

As newly arrived and least significant of the company I was required to say first what I had learned. I began with what I supposed would be common knowledge among us by now, keeping the more particular things to the end. The boy, Thomas Wells, was twelve years old and small for his age, not much given to smiling owing to the fact that he was frequently beaten by the drunken man his mother lived with. His own father was dead or gone away.

"The father walked off one fine morning," Springer said. He was sitting cross-legged but by some squirming motion of the body and by moving his shoulders first one, then the other, he was a man walking blithe and free. There was no smile on his face, however. "He went to join the wars they say. They said that about mine, but I never believed it."

"They are poor," Stephen said. "The man is in bondage of labor to the Lord de Guise. He has a strip of plowland, not more than three acres."

"He finds money for ale," Martin said. "He was drunk on the day the boy died. Drunk and quarrelsome. In the end the innkeeper would not serve him."

"Will we play that?" Springer's eyes were round. "Supposing he is there, among the people?"

"Devil take him, we will play it," Stephen said. "If he quarrels with me he will be the sorrier."

"He tries to pretend he is not drunk, so the innkeeper will serve him more ale. He gathers all his forces." Straw straightened himself and held his body in precarious balance and his head trembled in the effort to appear sober. Then he shivered, and it was a true shiver. It was cold in the barn, but I knew that Straw was frightened.

"The innkeeper waits," Martin said. "The man cannot sustain it, his legs turn to jelly." And he acted both in turn, the stare of the innkeeper and the collapse of the man and it was very comical.

"They had sold their cow," I said, when the laughter had stopped. "Poor they must be, to sell a heifer in winter. Their hay was spoiled with rain and they could not feed the beast through the spring. That was where the money came from that the boy was carrying. They must have sold it somewhere outside the town . . ."

"The beast was sold six miles away," Tobias said, "in a village called Appleton, on the edge of the moors. The man and woman stayed there, drinking in a tavern. At least the man drank and the woman stayed with him. She gave the money, as much of it as she could get hold of, to the boy for safekeeping and sent him home with it."

"But he never got home," Martin said. "He was seen in the afternoon, two or three miles along the way, by one gathering kindling at the border of the woodland."

"He was found half a mile outside of the town," Stephen said, "where the road runs below the common. I walked out to it. The way is narrow there, with the wood growing close on one side and the waste on the other, rising up to the common. The house where the woman lived is on the edge of the common, a little nearer to the town."

"She lived there with her father, who is a weaver," Straw said. "Why did they not take him also, if the money was found there?"

No one knew the answer to this.

"It was the Lord's confessor that saw her," I said. "The Benedictine." I paused, experiencing the pleasure of one about to impart something of moment. I was excited—we all were. Excited and afraid. These things had happened. Now with our words we made them happen again, as later we would with our bodies. "He saw the girl on the common land that evening. She was near the roadside at the place where the boy was found."

"What was she doing there?" Stephen said. "Was she waiting there for Thomas Wells? Perhaps she had seen him coming. The land rises there, you can see some way along the road."

"Why should she wait for Thomas Wells?" I said.

"In that case, the Monk would have seen the boy too," Martin said. His face showed something of that bright abstracted look it had worn when he first spoke to us of his idea. "It seems that the last one to see Thomas Wells alive was the man gathering wood, and that was some three miles from where he was found."

"That will be why the Monk went to the house," Margaret said, speaking now for the first time. "He saw her near the place, then when the boy was found, he remembered he had seen her and went there, to the house, and so found the money."

It is always difficult, when we look back with our minds, to be sure of a time when things became different, when a current darkened or brightened, when words or glances changed the mood. To my mind it was then that the shadow fell, while Margaret was speaking. I seem to remember some reddening of the light, as if the last poor glow of our fire was diffused round us and we sat there in this light while darkness thickened outside, and we were the same people but yet different. It was then we began to see that this matter was not so simple as we had thought. These three things concerning the Monk—seeing the woman, learning of the boy's death, finding the money—though they had seemed at first to explain everything, raised more questions than they settled.

"Perhaps there are others who saw her there," Martin said slowly. "In any case, it is common land, she could have had a dozen reasons for being there, and the Monk would have known that."

"How did the Monk come to be there, on the road?" Tobias said.

There was a silence, then Straw gulped and laughed and it sounded loud there in the barn. He was always sensitive to mood, more than any of us, and always excitable and wavering, like a weather vane, turning this way and that. "He would have been out on the Lord's business," he said.

I tried to picture the face of the Monk, whom I had never seen, to give him substance, but other faces came instead: Martin's face with the light of his idea on it, the streaked face of the idiot as he named the lost children, the scarred, disdainful face of the Knight as he rode by under his canopy. The Monk, though on the Lord's business, had yet had occasion to note, and to remember, a young woman seen for a few moments on the common land . . .

"How was Thomas Wells killed?" The question seemed to come from the midst of us, it was difficult for some moments to know who had uttered it. But it was Tobias, the practical one, the mender. "What was the manner of his death?" he said now, with some note of impatience in his voice.

"We do not yet—" Martin began.

"He was strangled," Margaret said. "Thomas Wells was strangled."

We looked at her as she sat there, her sturdy legs spread below the drab brown skirt. She had combed out her fair hair and tied it with a scrap of red ribbon.

"How do you know this?" Stephen said, his being the right to question her first.

"I found the man Flint," she said, raising her chin at him —there was a sort of defiance often in her movements. "The one who came upon the boy's body. He is a widower, a mild man enough. He lives alone."

There was silence among us for some moments. No one inquired into the means she had used to get this information from Flint. Then somebody—I think it was again Stephen—asked if it had been with a rope and she said no, the life had been taken from him with hands.

"Flint saw the bruises made by the thumbs," she said. "The boy's tongue was hanging out. Otherwise he was lying neatly on his back at the side of the road, out of the way of the carts."

"A boy of twelve," Martin said. "He would have fought for life. The woman will be strong."

"Perhaps she pounced upon him from some hiding place," Springer said and he glanced round the barn as if the place might be there.

Stephen shook his head. "There is no hiding place there near enough to the road. The woodland is lower down, fifty yards off."

"Perhaps she took him into the trees?"

"Why would he go with her?" Tobias said. "And if he did, and she killed him there, why should she bring him back to the road?"

No one could find an answer to this and again there came a silence among us. Then Martin raised his head and shook himself slightly, as if dispelling some vision. "So this is the story," he said, "at least as far as we know it. The man and woman go with the boy to the village of Appleton and there they sell their cow. The man starts drinking. The mother gives the money, let us say in a purse, to the boy, and bids him go straight home with it and speak to no one on the way. The boy sets off, but he never reaches home. He is seen on the road about three miles from the town by a man gathering wood. The woman is seen on the common land close to where the boy was found. She is seen by the Lord's confessor, who is out on the Lord's business. No one else sees her. This is in the afternoon, not far from the dark. But it is not until early next morning that the boy is found by this man Flint. He has been strangled and there is no purse anywhere about him."

He paused, looking at Margaret. "What was Flint doing there?" he said.

"He was going out to where his sheep are penned," she said. "He put the boy on the back of his mule and brought him into the town."

"Later that same morning the Monk learns of the murder. He makes his way to the house where the girl lives, taking with him some of the Lord's people as witnesses, or so I suppose. He finds the purse. The girl is carried off to the prison. In the course of that day and the next she is tried in the Sheriff's court, which in effect is the Lord's court, and she is condemned. She is condemned but not hanged yet."

He was silent for some moments, looking straight before him. Then, in low tones, he said, "There must be some reason for that. Everything else was done with such dispatch, even to the burying of the boy. He was laid in earth yesterday, scarce two days after he was found. Still, it serves our purpose, good people. While this is not yet done the interest in our play will be greater. We will be playing under the gallows tree."

This was a thing only Martin could have said and there was a kind of singleness of mind in it that belonged only to him among us. There were contradictions in him which puzzle me yet. Where it concerned his will he would set all else aside, and that is wickedness, whoever does it. He had no piety. And yet there was great tenderness in his nature, and loyalty to any who gave him trust.

"Perhaps they are seeking to make her confess, for her soul's sake," Springer said.

"I tried to learn whether she had confessed," I said. "The

one I asked took it at first for jesting, but he would give no
answer. There is a justice coming from York, he was expected last night at the inn. Perhaps they are waiting for
that."

"Certain it is that he is not the Lord's guest," Tobias said,
"or he would be staying at the castle." He hesitated for a
moment, then said, "There is one thing more . . . It does
not concern this murder, but I heard again the name of John
Goody, who it seems was of an age with the murdered
boy."

"Again?" Stephen raised thick eyebrows. "When did we
hear it before?"

"This morning," Springer said. "We heard it this morning. He was one of those the poor simple man spoke of, the
one who came to our fire. He spoke of seeing angels and
things too bright for his eyes." With this he raised his right
hand in imitation of the gesture the beggar had used, palm
outward, fingers spread, and the face peering behind this
screen as at some vision dazzling and enticing. "He was
wild in his talk, except for the names," he said. "Those were
clear enough."

"We have enough to do, without this," Martin said. He
spoke impatiently, but it did not seem to me that these
words expressed his feelings fully. However, it was true that
there was much to do. We had to make a procession
through the town and announce our play while there were
people still abroad.

We did it on foot, not wanting to risk the cart again. We
carried torches and went in a body, with no great clamor
this time, Martin having decided that we should make our
procession a solemn one, as if it were to the place of execution. We had to use Margaret to make up the numbers,
though this was consented to unwillingly on Martin's part,
as she was not of the company. She wore her usual ragged
finery of blue robe with slashed sleeves and on her face the

hideous mask of Avarice, cause of the crime. Stephen led the way as God, who sees all things, in his long white robe and tall hat and gilded mask. Springer wore a red dress and the same flaxen wig he used for Eve but his face now was bare, since the condemned must not be allowed any refuge or concealment. Round his neck was a noose and a short length of rope, which dangled before him. Tobias walked behind as executioner, in a sort of helmet with eyeholes that Margaret had made out of some black stuff. He had a drum slung below his chest and with his right hand, as we walked, he struck the drum with a single note, keeping time to the rhythm of our walking. Straw was Death, in a hooded robe, his face whitened with chalk paste. Martin had put on the Devil's mask, the one I had worn in the Play of Adam, and he skipped and danced to show that Hell was gleeful at the prospect of receiving this woman. I was Good Counsel, with little to do, since my counsel had been ignored, but make the gesture of sorrow from time to time. I had donned again, for this role, my clerical habit, last worn by Brendan and still, to my senses, bearing something of Brendan about it, though it had hung all night in the barn for airing. So I was a priest playing a priest, dressed for the part in my own dress. The boy, Thomas Wells, we did not show, not having yet decided how we would play him.

So to this solemn sound of the drum we proceeded, through the first driftings of a new snowfall. The flakes slanted down and spluttered faintly on our torches. The gesture of sorrow obliges one to look heavenward and my face was soon wet. I saw that Springer too had streaks of wet like tears on his face and this was because he too, as the condemned woman, had to raise his face toward the sky in order to implore mercy, a gesture which is stronger when done without movements of the hands. The demon danced, Death made sorties accompanied by the gesture of reaping and every so often Stephen stopped and we all stopped with

him and he cupped his hands to his mouth and called out
the Play of Thomas Wells and gave the hours for next day—
the first playing of it would be at noon. And the snow came
out of the dark, like a swarm of creatures attracted by our
light.

Doubts must have been drifting and twisting through our
minds even then, in the midst of our procession, while we
listened to the drumbeat and felt the snow on our faces and
paused to listen to God's shout. Only in this way can what
happened among us next day be explained.

We reached a place where streets crossed, one returning
leftward to the market square, the other leading out of the
town. Here, among a press of people, we were obliged to
wait. Liveried servants on horseback barred our way, edg-
ing their mounts sideways, blocking the street from wall to
wall. We stood there and waited. The people were all round
us and I did not know whether they had joined our procession or we had joined theirs. Some voice in the crowd said
this was the King's Justice that had come to town.

After some minutes they came passing before us, looking
neither to right nor to left, hooded and cloaked against the
snow, so that it was not possible to single out the Justice
from among his people. Tobias, who though patient enough
in his everyday manners, soon chafes at any restraint of
authority, struck the drum a single sudden blow and this
startled one of the horses so that it shied and the man cursed
us, and Tobias struck the drum again and then they were
past.

This had destroyed the rhythm of our procession and
mixed us with the people. Besides, the snow was thickening.
We took the shortest way back, following in silence behind
the more successful procession of the Justice, reaching the
inn while their horses were being stabled. The inn yard was
full of bustle but the Justice himself was nowhere to be seen.

We could not rest as we had now to practice our play. It

was to be done in the form of a Morality, using some set
speeches that the players knew already, each in his own
part, but depending much on gesture and dumb-show, with
lines interposed at the impulse of the players. Martin had
once seen Italian players in London make a play of this sort,
with some of the speeches habitual to the characters and
others interposed as seemed fit.

"If we are concentrated upon the action," Martin said,
"and with the masks making us more free, we can do much
for effect in this sudden way. It comes from the particular
moment and the people watching will be taken by surprise,
they will not know what to expect. Even if we do some
things clumsily, there will still be this surprise in it. But if
any of us takes it in mind to change the course of the story,
he must make the sign before, so the others will know it and
be ready."

I did not know this sign and it was shown to me: the hand
is turned at the wrist as if one were tightening a bolt and
one can do this slowly or rapidly and with the arm in any
position, so long as the twisting motion of the hand is evident.

In the bestowing of the parts we found some difficulty.
There were three actions in the Play of Thomas Wells: the
setting forth, the encounter on the way, and the finding of
the money. Six players were needed for this, without counting the Virtues and Vices. Some of us therefore had to
double parts. But the main difficulty concerned Springer.
Since he was only fifteen and short of stature it was clear
that he should play Thomas Wells. In fact he was the only
one of us that could do so. But this meant that he could not
take either of the women's parts, since both appeared before
the people at the same time as the boy.

"Straw will have to do it," Martin said. "He can do the
mother without a mask and the guilty woman in two masks
—an angel mask for the deceiving of the boy, and a demon

mask for the killing. We will have Avaritia and Pieta contending for the woman's soul. I will play the first of these and Tobias the second, as we know something about these parts already from doing the Plowman Interlude. I will play the Monk also. Stephen will play the drunken man in the tavern."

"A part very fitting," Margaret said. Since her disclosure concerning Flint she had gained in the general consideration, and no one reproved her, not even Stephen though he glowered.

"He will also be the retainer who accompanies the Monk to the girl's house," Martin said. "Nicholas will be Good Counsel. He makes a sermon to the boy to persuade him to stay on the road."

"You can put some Latin in it," Straw said, and he turned his eyes upward and intoned in a nasal voice: *"Hax, pax, max, Deus adimax.* What do you mean, stay on the road?" he said to Martin.

"The road is the way of life, turning aside for temptation is the way of death. We have done this before in Moralities. It is the only difference now that the death threatening the soul is also the death of the body. The woman tempts him with promises and he follows her."

"Follows her?" Straw laughed uncertainly. "But he didn't follow her. It was there on the road that he was found, poor soul."

Martin looked at him in silence for a moment or two. "No," he said quietly, "he must have gone with her, do you not see? It was not yet dark when they met together, there on the road. She had come down from the common, having seen the lad, or maybe for some other reason. There were people still about. The Benedictine had gone by shortly before. If it had been a blow, perhaps yes. But to kill the boy in such a manner, on the open road, while there was still light . . . No, she took him away to her house and did the deed there."

Straw shook his head. "That way she risked to be seen with him," he said.

"And afterward?" Stephen said. "She carried him back to the road in the dark of night?"

"She would know the ground," Tobias said. "All the same, it would be a heavy burden for a woman, and dangerous on the slope, she would not dare to show a light."

"Well, it must have been done so," Martin said. "There is no other way to think about it. She took him away somewhere. And as we must make a scene of it, we shall say it was her house."

This again was something only he among us could have said. In the silence that followed we all looked at him as he sat hunched forward there with his arms hugging his knees. It was as if we expected something more, perhaps some word of regret. But the face he turned to us, with its long narrow eyes and the sharp bones at cheek and temple, expressed nothing but its own certainty and indifference. He did not know where the woman had taken the boy; but they were persons in a play now and what mattered more to him than the truth of the place was the truth of the playing. "To bring him to the road again was a clever thing," he said. "It would seem some passerby had done it. Many use the road and where many are suspected the true culprit may well escape."

This was the version we decided upon and this is the way we thought to make our play. We practiced late into the night, going over the movements and the words. We were weary when we turned from it, but for long I could not sleep. There were vermin in the straw and I was cold, though wearing the Fool's headpiece and wrapped in Eve's robe over my habit. Martin and Tobias had blankets, and Straw and Springer shared one and slept together under it.

The rest of us made what shift we could with what we carried on the cart.

In the silence of the night the feeling of dread returned to me. I saw in my mind the woman with her burden, demons guiding her through the dark. These nights were starless, muffled in blackness by the snow clouds. But she had found her way, demons had guided her. The same demons that now were guiding us.

Nine

I WOKE AT FIRST LIGHT in the bitter cold. The fire was out and I heard Stephen groaning in some uneasy dream. Then there was silence and I felt the hush and knew there was heavy snow lying. I went out to void my bladder in the yard and the dog came with me, whimpering and snuffling as if it expected something from this rising and emerging of mine. As I came back to the barn I heard a cock crow and in the distance the barking of dogs. Two serving men in leather aprons came out into the yard with broom and shovel to clear away the new fall of snow. There was a stink of horses on the cold air and I saw a white slope of hillside beyond the roofs of the town. Afterward I remembered these things very clearly, with that longing we feel sometimes to recover a state of life that we have lost for ever, though perhaps that we have lost it is all its value.

It seemed like peace to me, that cold morning, with the hush of snow lying over the town and all the surrounding country. It is strange that it should have seemed so, because

I was in trouble enough already to any outward view, and my sins crowded upon me. I had left the transcribing of Pilato unfinished, I was outside my diocese without permission, I had sung in taverns and diced away my holy relics, I had lain with a woman in adultery, I had joined a troupe of traveling players, a thing expressly forbidden to clerics of whatever degree. In all this I had offended God and given pain to the Bishop of Lincoln, who had been like a father to me. And yet this was a time free of trouble compared with what was to follow upon our acting the Play of Thomas Wells.

I kept on the Fool's headpiece and covered myself as best I could with Eve's robe and sat inside with my back to the wall as the light strengthened and sounds and voices began to come from the rooms above. It entered my mind that I could get up, leave these scraps of travesty behind, and walk away into the quietness of the morning in my proper dress of a priest, as I had been when first I came upon them. My condition was the same: I was cold and hungry and penniless now, as then. But I was confused between the playing of the thing and the living of it, it grieves me to say it but I am resolved to tell the truth, the habit of a priest seemed travesty also, no less than the white robe that Stephen wore as God the Father or the horsehair suit of Antichrist. Or perhaps I was merely attached to my sin. In any case the moment passed.

I saw Straw's tousled head rise from the bundle it had been resting on and turn vaguely this way and that. There was no movement from Springer beside him. Margaret lay like one dead under a heap of red curtain cloth. Then Martin rose from his place and winced and muttered a little in the cold and bade me good morning. And so the day started.

The morning passed in practicing, though there was not space enough in the barn to do the movements properly.

Tobias and Margaret together fashioned an effigy of Thomas Wells with straw from the barn floor and twine and bits of clothing and they put on him the white mask that Straw sometimes wore when he played the Man of Fashion, and which has no expression, either of good or bad. This effigy it was necessary to make in order to show the change of death, also to make the burden light enough to be carried.

Martin was at first intending to do as we had done in the Play of Adam, that is to make our changes in the barn and come back again through the people. But Springer, who after his death as Thomas Wells was to be the angel that showed the Monk where the money lay hidden, would not agree to this. "I will not pass so close among them," he said. Springer was a fearful soul and like a girl in some ways: he felt no shame in showing that he was afraid. And the rest of us were secretly grateful for this, as the same fear was in all of us. Some measure of fear a player feels always because he is exposed to view and there is no shelter for him without abandoning the play; but now it was stronger, we knew that we would be coming close to the people's lives. So it was decided among us to make a space with curtains against the wall of the yard in the corner close to where we were playing.

When the noon bells began to sound we were still busy with this. The curtains were threaded through canes and the canes rested on corner posts, two of the sides being formed by the angle of the corner. While this work was being done by Stephen and Tobias and me, the others did tricks to entertain the people—there were already more folk in the yard than had come for our play of the evening before, and they were coming still. Straw and Springer did cartwheels, going different ways across, while Martin stood on his hands with a colored ball resting on the sole of each foot, one white, one red—the same that had been thrown to me as a test—and he walked on his hands over the icy cobbles, keeping his legs so straight that the balls did not roll off, a thing I had never seen in my life before.

Then our work with the curtains was finished and all of us save Martin and Tobias crowded into the room we had made and began to ready ourselves. Martin and Tobias continued some minutes longer before the people, one throwing up the balls and the other somersaulting to catch them. Then Tobias joined us. "The yard is full," he whispered. We stood there in the cramped space, listening first to the breathing of his exertions and then to the voice of Martin, as he began to speak the Prologue.

> "Good masters, we beg for your patience
> And also to give good audience
> To this our play . . ."

They were the lines agreed on, taken from the Interlude called Way of Life, with some changes to accord more with the tenor of our play. But when Martin had spoken them he did not come at once to join us but remained there before the people, which we had not known he would do, and I think he had not known it either. There was a silence of some seconds. No sound came from the people. And then he spoke again but in his own voice.

"Give us your attention, good masters. This is the present play of your town. It is yours, and that is a new thing, to make a play that belongs to a town. And this play does honor to your town, because it shows that wrongdoers are punished here with great speed of justice."

Inside our tent of curtaining we regarded one another mutely. Tobias was frowning as he prepared to put on the mask of Pieta. I saw that Straw's lower lip was trembling slightly. The others I did not look closely at but I think we were all in fear. I went to the curtain and opened the parting a little and looked out. At that moment the rim of the sun showed above the wall on the side toward the sea and a faint radiance fell across the yard and gleamed on the wet stones. There was a strange light on things, a snow-light, although the yard had been swept clear; and this light was gentle and at the same time pitiless: there were no shadows in it. It was as if the light of all the miles of snow outside had gathered here for our play. And it lay on the faces of the people as they stood close together there, dressed for the day of the fair, rough faces of laboring people, paler ones of servants and maids, with here and there the sharper or more stately look of people more well-to-do. These faces all were turned toward Martin and his voice filled the yard.

"When we make a play of a wicked act we give God's pity further occasion, for those who play in it and those who watch. So as you look for pity you will be ready to grant it to us poor players and to those whose parts we take." With a sudden gesture he raised his arms to the sides, palms outward to the people and raised above the shoulders. "Gentle people," he said, "we give you our Play of Thomas Wells."

He came back now to join us and his face was calm but his breath caught a little. Straw and Springer and Stephen stepped out to begin the play, Straw dressed in a country-woman's bonnet and padded out with straw inside his kirtle to make him buxom, Stephen in his own ragged jerkin—the one he had worn at our first meeting, when he had threatened me with his knife. Springer, as Thomas Wells, wore his own drab doublet and hose.

Tobias had fashioned a purse out of black felt, a good big one that all could see. And Stephen tossed it up so that the people should see it well, and he laughed in the manner of a boor, ho-ho-ho, with the hands held loosely clenched against the sides of the waist and the trunk of the body moved forward and back. Martin had schooled him in this and he did it well. There was laughter among the people to see a man laugh so at having made a bad bargain, because all knew that the cow had been sold out of need, and one or two called out, but not in anger as it seemed to me—if the man himself was there among them, he gave no sign of it. The laughter died away soon into silence and this quick dying away was a disturbing thing.

I watched through the curtain as the play went on. Things were done as we had planned and practiced them, the drunkenness of the man, the woman's filching of the purse, her miming of the dangers facing her son on his six-mile journey back to the town. Despite the full skirt and the bulk of his padding Straw succeeded well in miming the perils of bears and wolves and robbers, and Springer followed all these movements with a gooselike turning of the head to show his careful listening and good intention.

Then Stephen and Straw came back to change and I stepped out into the shelterless open and began my sermon to Thomas Wells.

"Good Counsel is my name and some call me Conscience, my task it is and also my delight to urge and prompt you and every man to keep well on the way of life, which way was opened for us by the sufferings of Christ . . ."

I said the words as they came to me, keeping my eyes steadily on Springer all the while, and making from time to time the gesture of exhortation, right hand raised and three middle fingers extended. There was some talking aside among the people and shifting of feet, they found the sermon long. Then there came again that sudden hush and I looked away from Thomas Wells and saw the woman come forward in the robe and wig and mask of the temptress— Straw had put on the round sun mask of the Serpent before the Fall.

For a moment I faltered in my lines. In that full un-shadowed light there in the yard, the scarlet robe and the yellow wig and the unchanging smile of the white mask

with its round pink cheek patches were very striking. I felt
my breath quickened as by some shock. And she did not
come nearer, but stayed at a distance and at first without
movement, while I continued my good counsel to Thomas
Wells, using now some set lines I had kept in my memory.

> "Of ghostly sight be you not blind
> On earthly store to set your mind.
> To give you life Christ suffered to be dead . . ."

But the eyes of the people were not on me. They were on
the woman, as she began her miming of delights. And this
again had been Martin's idea, for the woman to keep at a
distance and make a dumb-show of pleasures, while I still
continued with my sermon, so the words of spirit and the
gestures of flesh should contend together.

Martin's idea, yes; but Straw had made of it something
only he could do. Of all of us he was most gifted in playing.
Martin had high skill and a feeling for the spectacle and the
whole shape and meaning of the play far beyond any of us.
But there was in Straw an instinct for playing, or rather a
meeting of instinct and knowledge, a natural impulse of the
body, I do not know what to call it, but it is something that
can neither be taught nor learned. For the part of the temptress he had devised a strange and frightening way of bend-
ing the body stiffly sideways with the head held for a
moment in inquiry and hands just above the waist, palms
outward and fingers stiffly splayed in a gesture of his own
invention. So for a moment, while he made the pause to see
the effects of his tempting, he was frozen in wicked inquiry.
Then he broke again into sinuous motion, gesturing the
delights that awaited Thomas Wells if he would but follow:
cakes and pies and sweet drinks and the warmth of the
fireside and something more—there was some writhing suggestion of lewdness in it also.

This change from the flowing motions of pleasure to the

stiff pose of observing was a frightening thing, even to me who had seen him practice it alone in a corner of the barn. There was complete silence among the people. Looking toward the rooms above, I saw open casements and faces watching us, one of them a white face with a black cap fitting close and it came to me that this might be the Justice. I was coming now to the end of my exhortation.

"Sin in the beginning may seem full sweet
But the reckoning comes, be you never so fleet.
When you lie in clay . . ."

Thomas Wells stood between us in his simple dull-colored smock, looking from one to the other. His face was wide-eyed and solemn and he turned his body at the waist toward the one he looked at, keeping head and body in a straight line, and I saw the effort he made to breathe deeply enough and I felt his fear in me also, perhaps because of the silence —there was neither babble nor horseplay among the people, they sat hushed.

Straw too must have felt it. He was affected always by currents of feeling and unpredictable in his ways of responding. Now he did something that had not been at all in our practice. His movements before had been lascivious in some degree, and this more for the sake of the people than the boy. But now he moved his hands down the front of his body in a long movement of self-love and turned them to make the arrowhead shape and ran this arrow down the lines of the groin and held it there to show the form of the mons venereal, and he did this for Thomas Wells, swaying his body as he did it and it was a gesture of pride and power and terrible invitingness. I came to the end of my words as the woman still stood there showing the place of pleasure, and the stuff of the gown was strained over the fork of her body and showed the parts of a man beneath.

Thomas Wells went toward her, he too playing by impulse now, moving like someone between waking and sleeping, stepping high as if under a spell. I turned to the people and made the shrug of sorrowful resignation, with arms half-raised. But now, as the boy moved toward her, there was a sudden voice from among the people, a cry of anger or distress. A woman's voice—coming from the silence it had great force. Straw turned to see where the cry had come from and I heard the gasp of his breathing and saw the rise and fall of his breast. I stepped forward and lowered my head and made again the gesture of sorrowful resignation, hoping that this would give time for Springer and Straw to retire behind the curtain and prepare for the scene of the killing. But the woman called out again, and now with words. "It was not thus," she shouted. "My boy did not go with her." Her voice was loud, though there was the choke of tears in it. She was not looking at us, she was looking at those round her, which was worse. "My Thomas was a good boy," she shouted in appeal to them.

Other shouts came now from among the people. There was a movement among them, a rustle of violence. Danger of hurt for players comes like the sound of wind in the trees. Once heard it is never forgotten. The three of us were frozen there. We could not go on against the shouting, we could not retreat or the play collapsed. Then Martin came forward from behind the curtain and he had put on the hood of Mankind, but this he drew quickly back as he faced the people, turning his wrist as he did so in the sign of changing discourse. "Good people, why did he go with her?" he shouted. "Thomas Wells was not killed by the roadside."

This shouting above the people's shouts brought some moments of silence and Martin spoke loudly into the silence. His face was white, but his voice was confident and steady. "God's pity, not in such a manner as that," he said. "She would not do it there, on a road where people might pass." The silence held still. With the briefest of pauses he turned to me, arm extended in the gesture of indication. "You, Good Counsel, tell us why Thomas Wells gave you no heed."

I knew I must answer this quickly while we could be heard. I spoke the words as they came to mind: "Alas, good sir, man lives after his pleasure . . ."

Now, under Martin's eye, Springer made a memorable conquest of himself. He took some steps forward, making as he did so the gesture that accompanies the confession of Adam. "The woman tempted me and I did go with her," he said. As he spoke he turned toward Straw and fluttered the fingers of his right hand very briefly and rapidly, concealing this with his body from the view of the people. This sign I did not know at the time but it is the one that asks for a thing to be repeated by him you look at. "With her body she did me tempt," he said.

Straw drew himself up. The sun mask of the Serpent regarded us and all the people with its unfaltering smile. With the same sinuous movement as before the temptress caressed herself, made the arrow shape at the place of lust, swayed her shoulders in power and pride. And the silence among the people was again so complete that I heard the wings of a pigeon as it rose above the roof of the inn.

Now at last we were able to withdraw, all save Thomas Wells, who had to remain while Avaritia and Pieta prepared themselves to struggle for the woman's soul. And so we had been saved, and by our own exertions. But these same exertions, this narrow avoiding of disaster, set something free among us that had before been caged.

The first to show it was Springer, left alone there before the people. There is a sort of desperate boldness that comes to the fearful when they have gone beyond their fears and this it was perhaps that impelled Springer now. He had been intending, in order to lighten the mood of the people before the acting of the murder, to do the old mime of the thief of

eggs whose eggs break inside his clothes. It was this that he
had practiced and he had made us all laugh with it in the
barn. But instead he began to speak directly to the people.
Standing there together, we heard his voice, high-pitched
and clear, still with something of a child in it. We heard him
ask a question which, simple as it was, had not occurred to
any of us.

"Read me a riddle, good people," we heard him say.
"How did the woman know I bore the purse about me? Did
some demon whisper it to her? Did I toss it up and down as
I walked along? If I did so, would she have seen what it was
from where she stood on the common at the close of a
winter day?"

Stephen bent his large frame to peer through the parting
in the curtain. "He is walking back and forth before them,
tossing up the purse," he said in a hoarse whisper. His dark
eyes looked larger than usual, more prominent in his face.

"Go out and speak to him, Stephen," Martin said, "before they turn to anger again. Say what comes into your
mind to say. Then Tobias and I will come out for the scene
of argument."

Stephen was less able as a player but he had a quality of
hardihood that stood him in good stead now. He was in full
command of his voice and his nerves as he advanced on
Springer. Even without God's gilding he had a dignified
presence, and this despite his ruffian's nature. "Thomas
Wells, you boasted of it," he said in his deep voice. "You
boasted to the woman of the purse . . ."

We heard Springer make the crowing sound of false
laughter, then a voice came from among the people, a man's
voice, harsh and loud: "Fool player, what brought her near
enough to hear the boy boast?"

But now Avaritia and Pieta came forward with the
woman between them and they walked slowly back and
forth, halting to speak the lines, then resuming. The Battle

for the Soul is usually done with the players always in the same place and speaking in turn. But Martin had wanted more movement in it and had practiced Tobias in this walking and halting.

So we proceeded for some time, keeping to the way we had practiced. But we were not the same people as those who had practiced . . . Straw's changing of the masks succeeded well and was very startling to the people. He did it behind the backs of Avaritia and Pieta who came forward and stood side by side together facing the people and spread their cloaks, white for the Virtue, black for the Vice, then they drew aside to left and right and the woman was revealed with the demon's mask and she raised her hands and hooked the fingers and hissed at the people and some hissed back. This was to show that the Evil One had triumphed. The sun mask she hid in the waist of her gown.

The strangling of Thomas Wells was done in dumb-show. Straw did it alone before the people, without the boy. It was decided thus among us in whispers behind the curtain. Martin was for keeping it as we had intended, with the boy strangled in full view, as it made a strong scene, and this mattered more to his zealot's soul than the danger. But the rest were opposed—we were unwilling to rouse the people against us for a second time. So we passed directly to the bearing of the effigy back to the road and thence to the finding of the money.

This scene of the finding did not play so well as we had thought. Some things have better success in the practicing than in the playing. Martin as the Monk did what he could, hunting here and there, holding up the purse triumphantly when found, while Straw, still in his demon mask, cowered back against the wall. Despite this there was a lack of force and all of us felt it. It may be that what happened next was due to our sense of this lack and our wish to make it good. Or perhaps it was because Martin had to conceal the purse in his sleeve until it was found, there being nowhere else in that bare place to conceal it. It was Stephen as the Monk's servant that began it, and this too in a way was surprising, because though truculent in debating, he was the one least likely to undermine the form of the play once this had been agreed on. Being shouted at for a fool may have rankled in his mind, though he never admitted this. When he spoke it was in rhyme, and so it was with all of us, and the rhymes came easily, unhesitating, unforced—we were possessed.

Martin was holding up the purse in triumph. Stephen was making the gesture of indication toward it, which is done with the right arm held at fullest extent. Straw was cowering back in guilt and fear. I had come from behind the curtain in order to make a homily to the people on the theme of Divine Justice. Tobias came behind me in the mask of Pieta, wringing his hands and lamenting. The effigy of Thomas Wells lay before us on the wet cobbles, his white mask looking toward the people with no expression either of good or bad. Suddenly, without any sign or warning, Stephen lowered his arm, took two steps toward the people, and spoke:

> "Gentles, after deed so fell
> Why not hide the money well?"

At once, as if this had been a speech awaited, Straw straightened himself and with a rapid gesture removed his mask and showed a staring face below it.

> "Who knows the riddle, he can tell.
> What brought the Monk to that place?"

Pieta, behind me, had ceased lamenting. After a moment he spoke and I heard the tremor in his voice and knew from the clearer tone that he too had removed his mask.

"For he saw the woman's face."

Without any previous agreement among us and without being properly aware of how it was managed, we were all five of us now standing side by side facing the people, and the effigy of the boy lay there before us. And I felt a quaking within me and overcame it and spoke:

"In cold her face she would not bare
In winter cold a hood we wear . . ."

I saw the ranks of faces before me and the faces looking from the gallery above. My sight was blurred, all these faces ran together, there was noise from the people. Martin was in the midst of us with two on either side. He raised the purse once again and held it high in that same gesture of triumph. But there was a difference now and the difference was terrible. There was blasphemy in it. He played it like the supreme moment of the Mass, holding up the black purse with both hands at the fullest reach of his arms as if it were the Host, and he shouted against the muttering of the people:

"They only search who hope to find
Where it lay was in my mind . . ."

We had meant to close with a tableau of the execution, but it was clear now to all of us that we had reached the end of the Play of Thomas Wells. We waited a moment longer, then went all together and passed behind the curtain and stood there in silence. The faces of my companions were affrighted, as if they had seen some vision or woken from a dream of misfortune, and I supposed mine to be the same. The curtain that concealed us, though threadbare enough, was a protection. None came to offer us harm. Gradually the noise grew less as the people left the yard. Still we stood there, without moving or speaking. This trance was broken by Margaret, who came with the money. We had taken ten shillings and sixpence halfpenny, more than any could remember taking for a single performance ever before.

It was money that drew us on, or so at least it seemed then. I remember how we stood there and gaped at it. Time has gone by, it is difficult now to be sure whether it was the money or some other force that used the money as a lure. If the Powers contended for our souls that day it might have seemed that Avaritia had the victory in the battle for us as well as for the woman. But it was the winter season, there were still some days of journeying on bad roads, with a likelihood of starving in good earnest. It is not surprising that the money was a lure to us. In any case, I dare to say that we were not different in this from the Monk, the Lord's confessor, Simon Damian, as we later found to be his name —he in whose person Martin held up the purse of money as if it were the Heavenly Host at that strange ending of our play. For why was he there, at the castle, in attendance on the family of de Guise, but to secure grants and privilege for his Order, quite undeserved as the monks no longer obey the precepts of their Rule, which commands absence of private property, abstinence from butcher's meat, steady manual labor, and strict confinement within the monastic precincts. They own horse and hound and weapons, they eat their fill of beef and mutton, their servants do the work in the fields, they go abroad on business, like this one. Strange to think that, as also with Brendan, I never saw his living face . . .

Margaret came behind the curtain with the money in a box. We were still standing there, all six of us, standing close together. Straw's eyes were starting from his head and Springer was flushed and tearful. There was sweat on Martin's brow despite the cold, but his eyes shone when he saw the money. "Now we can put our own shillings into the

Monk's purse," he said—he still held it in his hand. "Good people, you never played better in your lives."

Margaret had taken the box up to the gallery and asked money from people looking down at the play. More than three shillings had come from this. "The Justice spoke to me," she said, and in the flattery of this her mask of indifference had melted away, her face looked younger and she raised her head and opened her mouth wider as she spoke. "He asked me questions," she said. "He kept me talking long. He said I was good-looking and should do well."

"He knows a whore when he sees one," Stephen said.

Below the sunburn of many years, Tobias's face was ashen now and his lean jaws were set hard. "Brothers, we have started something up here," he said. "Let us take the money and go. I knew it was folly from the start."

"You were the first to speak for it," I said and he glared at me. We were all in that state of exhaustion where an embrace or quarrel seem equally natural.

"Why did Good Counsel not keep to the play?" he said. "You were in the playing space. But instead you ranted out some tale of cold weather and a hood."

"I did not rant," I said. "It was Stephen that began it with his question to the people about the hiding of the money. Then Straw followed without giving any time."

But it was useless to try and deal out blame. Something had entered into us and we all knew it.

"What questions did the Justice ask you?" Martin said.

"He asked the place we had come from and where we were going. He asked whose had been the idea to play the murder and how we had learned so much of it in so short a time."

"And you, what did you say?"

"I told him what he asked. Why should I not? I told him the idea was yours and he asked your name and I told him. Where is the harm?"

Martin smiled. "There is no harm," he said. "You did well to take the box up, Margaret."

"And we would all do well to get clear of this town while we may," Springer said.

Martin was still smiling. "Get clear of the town?" he said. "But we have promised to do the play again."

We looked at him as he stood there, smiling in the reddish light that strained through the curtains, with the empty purse in one hand and the box of money in the other. I could see no particular expression on anyone's face. We were beyond surprise, I think, now.

"Do the play again?" Stephen said. "How promised? You mean when we shouted it out? Shouting out a play does not make a promise."

"We have taken more than ten shillings," Martin said. "We will take more tonight."

"But we have enough," I said. "We have enough already to get to Durham, more than enough."

"We could take as much again," Stephen said, and he made the sign of money, which is done by opening and closing the hand very rapidly. That it should be Stephen to speak so soon in favor of staying was not a surprising thing, at least it does not seem so to me now. He was robust in body but in imagination weak, and coarse in his sensing of things.

"As much again? We will take twice as much," Martin said. "The fame of our play will spread. And in the dark, with the torches set against the walls . . ."

"God pity us, it would make a fine show," Straw said. Players are strange creatures. Still pale and shaken as he was, he clapped his hands at the thought of it, which was the thought of himself playing in it. Straw never looked much beyond his own part.

"We will buy good leather and Tobias will mend our shoes so we have dry feet on the way," Martin said. "Margaret can have stuff for a new gown. We will have good lined cloaks against the weather, each of us his own, and meat and ale over all the Christmas time. You will have game pie, Springer."

Poor Springer smiled at this, still with traces of tears on his face. Thus, once again he won us over. But there was more to it than money and I think we knew this already in our hearts.

"The play is not the same now as it was," Straw said. "And we are not the same, the parts have changed."

"The Monk would not have seen her face," Tobias said with sudden loudness. "Herding goats is cold work, Nicholas was right, she would have worn a shawl or a hood." And he smiled at me and nodded and we were friends again.

"Perhaps he knew her from her dress," Springer said.

"That would argue that he knows her well," Martin said. "How well does he know her, the daughter of a poor weaver?"

"How well does she know him?" Stephen said.

"Is that why she came down to the road?" Springer said. "Not seeing the boy, but seeing the Monk?"

"There is woodland not far on the other side," Stephen said. "I went there to see. It would make a meeting place."

I have said it before, we were possessed. We saw the danger as it came nearer but we could not draw back from this game of guessing, we could not pause from it. I too played my part, I said my lines as the prompter bade me. "He was riding alone," I said. "There was no one with him."

"If she came down to see the Monk," Straw said, "where then was the boy, where was Thomas Wells? Did he see them together?"

"We must learn more," Martin said. "Then we can make a play they will talk about in this town for ever."

His face was pale, the fair skin almost transparent, the

mouth with its full underlip compressed as it was in his moods of excitement or exaltation. No one argued further. We were still standing in that close circle, like plotters about to take an oath. Then Straw shivered and clutched at himself. "It is madness," he said and I saw Springer take his hand.

"We must learn more," Martin said again. "We must go out again into the town." He looked directly at Margaret. "Can you find the man Flint again, the one who found the boy?"

"I can ask for him," she said. "I know his house." She paused a moment, then said, "He saw our play, he paid his penny at the gate."

"Can you do again what you did with him before and ask him in return a question?"

"What question is that?"

"Ask him, when he found the boy, whether he can remember if the body was frosted."

"Frosted?"

"Yes, yes," he said, with sudden impatience. "Ask him whether the boy's clothes were whitened over with frost and was this a light frost or were his clothes stiffened with it. It was early morning when he was found, not much after first light. All those days the ground was hard with frost. Do you remember when we were talking of what to do with Brendan? We had to bring Brendan here because we could not bury him in that hard ground without mattock and spade."

"The reason we brought Brendan here was that you wanted a church burial for him." Stephen bore grudges long and he had seen an opportunity to give this one an airing. "Then we had to pay the priest," he said. "Then we had to make this play to get back the money."

"And have we not done so? Brother, what you say may be true, but it does nothing to change the fact that there was a deep frost in those mornings. If the boy lay all night by the roadside with no shelter but the dark, there would have been ice in the corners of his eyes, the folds of his clothes would have been stiff with frost. If not, he must have been taken there or killed there early in the morning, not very long before Flint came upon him."

"Early in the morning? But who would be by the road then?"

"The one that killed him," Martin said. In the silence that followed upon this, he looked round at our faces. "We will go and find out something more," he said. "The play we gave was the false play of Thomas Wells. Tonight we will give the true one. And so we will shout it to the people. And tomorrow, when we leave for Durham, every one of us shall have money enough for a month."

Money enough for a month. For poor players that is money enough for ever. It comes to me sometimes again, his triumph as he held up the purse with both hands, in the very gesture of the celebrant priest. How far did he believe what he told us? He talked of true and false but he did not mean these words as they are commonly meant. He wanted a play with strong scenes, one that would disturb the people and send them away changed. Is that a true play? And he wanted money. He won us over, but to win us over was his role. He was prompted in the lines that he spoke, as were we all. Some fascination of power led us to imprison ourselves in this Play of Thomas Wells.

Ten

WE WENT our separate ways again into the town. No one said to the others what he would do. I went into the marketplace, which was loud with hens and geese and traveling tinkers shouting their wares. The snow was trodden and churned between the stalls and there were piss marks in it and feathers and scraps of kale and carrot. The sky was clear and pale with loose shreds of cloud in it like the clippings of sheep. A man on stilts passed through the crowd shouting that the town bathhouse had good hot water. There was a ragged man kneeling in the snow and juggling with three knives.

I saw the beggar who had come to our fire and spoken of lost children. An egg had fallen and smashed below the stall, where the snow was trodden. The yolk of the egg made a yellow smear on the snow and a rawboned dog saw it at the same time as the beggar did and both made for it and the beggar kicked the dog, which yelped and held back but did not run, hunger making him bold. The beggar cupped his hands and scooped up the egg in the snow and took it into his mouth and ate all together, the egg and the fragments of shell and the snow. He saw me watching him and smiled the same smile, with the wet of the snow and egg glistening on his innocent face. I remembered then that he had been ready with names, as if in that simplicity of his mind names were like a lesson learned, and I approached him and asked him the name of the woman's father. He said it at once, smiling still: "His name is John Lambert, good master. The father of the one to be hanged is called John Lambert."

I gave him a penny and he turned away with the coin clenched tight in his left hand. As he did so, very briefly, he raised his right hand and held it before his face in that same gesture of dazzlement. "She would tell where the others are, if she could be brought to speak," he said. Then he went shambling away from me and I lost sight of him among the people.

She lives on the edge of the common . . . Someone had said that, the day before when we were talking among ourselves. *Her father is a weaver* . . . I thought he would more probably be abroad on this day of the market but there was a chance I might find him at home and I had no other idea of what to do. However, it was of no use to present myself to him either as priest or player. Then it occurred to me that I could pretend to be a clerk of the Justice. Quite by chance I had taken the black cloak of Avaritia to wear when we came out from the barn, that being the only thing left that offered any protection from the cold. And I was wearing the round black hat that I always wore abroad to cover my shorn head.

I made my way out of the marketplace and on to the road that led out of the town, going past that meeting of ways where we had been held back by the mounted men the evening before and seen the Justice ride by with his retinue. A path led up from here, skirting the common. Snow lay over the fields, unbroken. The crystals glinted on the slopes as I climbed upward. The skins of the beech trees that ran along the rises at the edge of the common had their silver darkened by this whiteness of snow and the sheep looked dirty against it.

I remember this walk well. It seemed for the moment that I was free and on the road again, without this incubus of the boy's death. I mounted the slopes quickly and I felt the youth of my blood. I had tied scraps of canvas round my shoes and bound my legs with cloth below the knee, as had we all before setting out, and my feet had so far kept dry enough. I saw the tracks of a trotting fox leading away into the shrub.

I met a man carrying a bundle of dried gorse twigs on his back, kindling he had raked out from the heart of the bushes, where it keeps dry, and I asked him if he knew the house of John Lambert. I thought he looked at me strangely and wondered if he remembered my face from the play. But my cloak was voluminous, as was necessary for Avaritia, it would have covered two of my size, and it was of an antique cut. And the human regard is strange in any case. He pointed higher, to a stone-built cottage enclosed in a timber fence. It was a house with byre and living place side by side and the entrance in the middle. Smoke came thinly from a hole in the thatch. I went through into the yard and geese lowered their heads at me and set up a clamor. I called out and waited there, on the slate flags below the step. The snow had been swept clear and there was a skin of dried blood on the slate where a pig had been killed. After some moments of waiting I heard the wooden bolt drawn back and a tall, gaunt-faced man stood at the threshold looking at me without great friendliness.

"What is it?" he said. "What do you want with me?" His voice was strong, with some hoarseness in it, as from much use.

"I am sent by the Justice that is come to town," I said. "He wishes to be satisfied of your daughter's guilt. I am sent to inquire further into the matter and bring back a report."

His eyes moved slowly over my person, the hat, the cloak, the scraps that bound my feet and legs. They were pale eyes, almost colorless, as if bleached, and they were set deep in his head. "From the King's Justice," he said. "Well then, come in."

It was almost as cold within the house as without. A small fire of wood chips was burning in a brick hearth in the middle of the room and the smoke of it hung in the air. His loom stood close to the single window and his narrow pallet was set against one wall. There was a door beyond, which I supposed gave admittance to the room where the woman had slept.

The Weaver stood looking at me. There was a high-backed chair in the room but he did not ask me to sit. The frame of his body was big, but he was wasted, either from illness or underfeeding. He raised his hands and flexed the fingers, which were dark red with cold. They were thick, strong fingers—strong enough to choke the life from boy or man. He filled the room in some way, there was a sense in me of not having enough space. I clutched the cloak about me, not wanting him to see Brendan's ragged doublet below it. "I am sent by my master," I said, "to inquire into the facts of that morning when the Lord's chaplain came here to your house and found the stolen money. There is a question as to why—"

"The Monk found no money here." The words came unhurried, with that slight hoarseness in them. It was a voice that was used to talking. Without taking his eyes from me he gestured round the bare room. "Look round you, my young man that is sent by the Justice. Having stolen money and killed to steal it, would you hide it in your own place when there are fields and woods all round?"

"But the purse might have been well hidden even here," I said. "Being suspicious, they came prepared to search."

"They came prepared to find," he said. "What is the name of your master, the Justice?"

I had not anticipated such a question, being unused to deceit. "Stanton," I said—the first name that came to mind. "His name is William Stanton." The pause had been too long but he gave no sign of noticing anything amiss. He continued to regard me in the same lingering manner, but with a strange dispassion now, as one might look at a drifting leaf or an odd-formed cloud in the sky. I was disconcerted by this and I blundered. "Where exactly was the money found?" I asked him.

He was silent for a moment, then he said, but quite calmly, "All this was deposed before the Lord's Sheriff by that devil's scum of a Benedictine. The Justice can see the writings if so he wishes. It is not necessary for a man to come here through the snow to ask me such a question. You seemed uncertain of your master's name. Can you tell me the name of the Monk?"

I could not answer this, and looked at him without speaking.

"Simon Damian is his name and God will find him out," he said. "You are not come from the Justice, brother, are you?"

"No," I said, "it is true that I am not."

"God reveals all lies to me because He is all truth and He dwells within me," he said in the same tone. "The Children of the Spirit share in the nature of God. I knew from the first you were not what you said. If I had thought it true I would have not opened my lips."

I began to speak but he cut me short. "I would say nothing to one that came from a justice," he said. "The justices are like the priests, spawn of hell, ravening wolves that harry the sheep and feast on the blood of the poor. But the time will come, the people will turn. I say to the people, be of good heart, do as the wise husbandman who gathered the wheat into his barn but uprooted the tares and burned them." He looked at me now and his pale eyes had a light in them. "We know these tares," he said. "Let them take heed, let them beware, for the time of the harvest is coming."

I was tempted to reveal to him that I was a man in Orders and therefore knew better than he where God makes His dwelling. But had I done so he would have put me out. All the same I was unwilling to allow such heresy to go unreproved. And by arguing against him it seemed to me that I would make more space for myself in that room. The Weaver had a strong presence and he was somehow taking all the air from me.

"It is not for us to judge who is for burning," I said. "God is the judge and He dwells apart. Brother, you did not find me out because God dwells within you, but because I did not lie well enough. If I had been a better liar you would have believed me." Thus I turned my falsehood to God's service, asserting His entirely separate being. It did not occur to me until later that I might have done better to keep silent and repent my lies. "Man's nature is corrupt," I said, "and has been so since loss of Eden. He may be redeemed, but God is nowhere to be found within him. Our way to redemption is through Holy Church, there is no other way. *Ex ecclesiam nulla salus.*"

"You talk like that servant of Antichrist who came here and took away my girl and left me with the goats and geese to tend as well as my loom," he said. "Have you come from him? Are you too one of the host of Antichrist? You are in borrowed robes and that is a sign of it." He spat aside and made the sign of the Cross. "Whoever you are," he said, "and whoever sent you, I say again there was no money found here. They hate me because I travel abroad, bearing witness and speaking against the rich and the priests. They

know their days are numbered . . . They seek to bring me
before the judges but they are afraid of rousing the people if
they do it without good cause. A spark is all that is needed
now. I am one of the forerunners. As tares are gathered and
burned in the fire, so shall it be at the end of the world, and
the wicked shall howl in Hell for ever."

"But it is not you who have been taken," I said. "It is she,
your daughter, who is under sentence of death."

"Me? How could they take me?"

For a moment I thought he was claiming God's special
protection. I was about to speak but he raised a hand to stay
me—the gesture of the orator postponing interruption, arm
bent at the elbow and held up at a slight angle with the palm
facing outward. I resolved to remember it. "You know
nothing of it," he said. "You are a stranger here. Why do
you come asking me questions?"

Then I told him I was a player, that we wanted to make
the True Play of Thomas Wells, and we were trying to find
out the true things that happened so as to show them to the
people.

"You would show it in a play?" he said. "You would
make a play of a true thing?"

"We can show it to be true by making a play of it," I said.

It was clear from his face that he thought this a damnable
proceeding, which I could well understand as I partly so
regarded it myself. He paused for some moments with lowered head, looking somberly before him. "And you would
show this devil's pander of a monk, this Simon Damian, you
would show him . . . One of you would play him before
the people?"

"Certainly."

"Players are a brood of Satan," he said in a considering
voice.

"We will make a true play of it," I said, "as far as we can
know the truth."

"Well," he said, "we set thieves to catch thieves. I will tell you. It was for me that they came. They came to find the money in my house, but I was not here."

"Where were you?"

"I was at the house of friends in the hamlet of Thorpe, three hours' walk from here. I stayed the night there. There were brethren of the Spirit come from far—they had come from Chester. We stayed together in the house, praying and bearing witness. There are many who can vouch for this. I told it to the Lord's Sheriff but it availed my daughter nothing, the Monk denied that it was for me he had come."

"So when he came there was only your daughter in the house?"

"Yes, only my daughter."

"And he did not know this?"

"How could he know it? If he had known it he would not have come."

"But that takes us in a circle," I said, offended in my sense of logic.

"Listen, master-player or Devil's messenger or whatever you are. They have wanted to take me for years past because I speak against the monks and friars and especially against the Benedictines, most slothful and debauched of all. This Simon Damian is a minister of Hell, he serves the Lord and helps him to live delicately on our labors and goods. We starve while they feast, we groan while they dance. But they will groan in their turn when the day—"

"What will be done with them?" I said.

"They will burn," he said. He stared before him as if he saw the flames already there. "They will be put to the fire, with their hounds and horses and their whores that they feed and clothe from our labors. Also the Jews will be put to the fire, who crucified Christ and live by breeding money. Also the clothiers and merchants of cloth will be put to the fire, who fix the prices among them and deny to the weavers the fruits of their labor. Why would he come only for the girl, and she afflicted? How does that serve his turn?"

"Afflicted?"

"I have work to do," he said bitterly, and he gestured toward the loom.

"When the Monk found the money, he still believed you were there somewhere in the house or nearby?"

"If he had not believed so, he would never have found it." Again I felt my mind bruise against the rock of the Weaver's logic. Everything came round in a circle back to him. He was privy to all schemes, the Monk's for convicting him of murder, God's for the punishment of the rich.

"By then it was too late," he said. "Someone they had to take, the money once discovered."

"Is your daughter also a Child of the Spirit?"

"She cannot bear witness," he said. "She came sometimes with me to meetings of the Brethren."

I turned to go. "What is her name?" I said.

"Her name is Jane." His face had softened with the uttering of it. "It was also the name of my mother," he said. "My wife and one son died in the plague and my older son died two years later in the famine of that year, when we all nearly died. More here died of want than of disease." His voice quickened and the lids lifted from his eyes as he stared at me. "My curse on him that took her and left me alone," he said. "May he die in blood. My curse on them that feast while we toil and pay us by the piece instead of letting us sell our own cloth and plunder the people of God. The Reckoning is coming, the time is near . . ."

At the door I glanced back. He had not moved. I met his eyes and I seemed to see the glint of tears in them. But his voice was the same, practiced, hoarse with much speaking. "She cannot bear witness," he said. "But I know her. She would hesitate to kill a mouse, or a wasp that had stung her, let alone a human child."

Eleven

I WENT BACK through the snow, thinking about the Weaver and his words. A wind was springing up, whipping the loose snow into drifts. I was intending to return to the inn and so took the way through the market, this being the shortest. The bells were ringing and some of the traveling people were taking down their stalls. It was not yet dark but the light was fading and the air was turning colder. I saw Martin standing below the platform of a man selling cures. He did not see me until I was there at his shoulder, being quite absorbed in listening. "We could learn something from this fellow," he said. "Look how he speaks and moves and keeps his pauses. He has the people in thrall to him, he persuades them they can buy immortal life for twopence."

There was some quality of excitement in the way he spoke, more than belonged to the subject. "Since we have met thus," he said, "you can go with me."

"Go with you where?"

"We are going to see the woman," he said. "We are going to the prison, Nicholas. Come, we can go now. The bells have started."

And as we walked back through the market he told me. There was an overseer of the prison and two keepers. The one whose turn came now Martin had spoken to and for a shilling he would admit one person, allow him to enter the cell and talk to the woman, so long as he himself was present at it. And he would say nothing of it to anyone.

"That last promise we can trust," Martin said. "It would be more than his place is worth to speak."

"A shilling?" I said. It was a week's wages for a jailor. "Out of the common stock?"

"Yes, yes, a shilling," he said with sudden angry impatience. "This is not a time for counting pennies. What should I do, seek you out and hold a meeting?"

He stopped there at the edge of the market and turned to me. "Did we not all agree?" he said. "We sat round and every man had his say. Did we not agree and set our hearts together in good accord that we should make the true play of the boy's death?"

I nodded, but he was wrong to say there had ever been rational assembly among us. Certainly we had agreed. We had entered upon it—like entering a walled place and not finding again the door which would let us out.

"It is a shilling well spent," he said. "We shall get the girl's account of it."

The wall of the prison was blank on the side facing the street. An alley ran alongside and there were steps leading up to a heavy door. Above the lintel, carved in stone, was a coat of arms, a leopard couchant and three doves in diagonal line. We sounded the iron knocker and waited and after some moments the ill-favored face of the jailor looked at us through the small grid that was set in the door. He smiled at the sight of Martin and opened the door to us.

We passed down a passage and crossed a walled courtyard with empty stables down one side and a sun-clock in
the middle. Then there were again passages and finally steps
leading down to the dungeons below ground where prison-
ers were kept. A voice and a rattle of chains came from the
dimness as we passed.

"Who are these kept in here?" I asked him, feeling horror
at the damp and darkness of the place.

He held up his lantern, grinning at us, showing a mouth
of ruined teeth. "Guests of the Lord de Guise," he said.
"This house is his. They are two that left his lands without
permission. This is done now on every hand, but Sir Richard is one that upholds the law. No man escapes him who
has done him any wrong. These two asked for higher wages
and when this was denied by the Lord's right, they left his
land and went to work for one who offered more. He sent
armed men to bring them back."

"And the landowner they had gone to? The one who gave
them the wages they asked, what of him?"

The jailor stopped near the end of the passage and spat
on the stone flags. "What could he do?" he said with contempt. "An old man with no living issue, a hundred acres of
land, a steward, a dozen men-at-arms . . . They fired his
woods to teach him not to poach labor."

"And that strikes you as a just proceeding?"

The jailor spat again and looked at me in ugly fashion.
He was a burly fellow with marks of old wounds on his
face. Only the thought of his shilling kept him civil toward
us. It was this he asked for now, holding out his hand for it.

"Where is the woman?" Martin asked.

"She is here." The jailor jerked his thumb toward the end
of the passage, where a faint light lay at the edge of the
stone flags. "In the end cell. An order came to give her
light . . ." His hand closed over the shilling. "Now you
can have your parley," he said, and a smile came to his face.

"You have paid dear for the pleasure of hearing your own crowing."

He moved forward and unlocked the door with a heavy key from his belt. "You," he said to me, "you stay outside here with me. It is he who pays, my word was to him. You can watch, if you have a mind to, from the door here."

He spoke as if a spectacle were promised. There was a sliding panel at head height in the door. Martin went into the cell and the door was closed and I watched through this opening. There was a candle-lamp with a glass guard set in a bracket on the wall and this gave out a pallid light. The cell lay below the street; I could hear the sound of the wind outside and small puffs of snow came through the grill of the high window and drifted slowly down into the light. The flame of the lamp, though guarded, flickered slightly and shadows moved over the walls.

Martin advanced with his light step into the room. "I come as a friend," he said. The Weaver's daughter stirred against the wall and I heard the sound of sliding metal and saw that she was chained by one ankle, though on a chain long enough to allow movement across the room.

I heard Martin's voice again, saying his name, and then from the woman a sound like no human voice; and I realized at that moment, as Martin must also have done, the significance of the jailor's smile as his fingers closed over the money: the woman's tongue could not make the shape of words.

I saw Martin check himself and stand still. "Can you hear what I say to you?" he said. There was kindness in his tone but nothing of pity. She turned toward him and raised her head and the light fell on her shoulders and face and the dark tangles of her hair. The eyes were in shadow but I saw the gleam in them. Her mouth was full-shaped without grossness, she was tender-lipped even in that wretchedness, even as she uttered more of those strange-pitched sounds which were all her throat could manage and which she could not hear.

I heard the jailor chuckle at my shoulder. Then Martin broke into mime, first with the snake-sign of tonsure and belly, then the flexing of fingers to show money, then two quick steps and the twisting movements of search and find. This done, he took up the posture of question, head tilted stiffly to the left, right hand held at waist level with thumb and forefinger extended. And in all these movements he was aped by his humpbacked shadow on the wall.

Her gestures in reply were rapid, too much so for me always to follow. I saw her shake her head and make the sign of the circle, not that slow one that indicates eternity, but hasty and repeated and made with both hands meeting and parting above and below. I did not know this sign, and perhaps it is not one that belongs to players. After it she took some steps away from the wall and the chain sounded on the stone floor. She stopped a yard from him and struck the palm of her left hand sharply with the forefinger with the right, which I took for a sign of truth-telling.

Martin made the sign of carnal relation, not that brisk one of copulation but the one that also suggests affectionate feeling, fingers interlaced and held straight. Again I think this is a sign only players use, for she did not know it and signified so by frowning and beckoning. He made the sign again, this time also setting his mouth in the shape of kissing. She made a violent gesture of denial, like a sideways blow with the flat of the hand, and I saw her eyes flash—it may have been true what her father said, that she would not harm the meanest of God's creatures, but there was a fire of anger in her. It was there in the movements of her body, in the sudden spreading of her hands before her, as at something unclean, to show her repugnance for the Monk.

The two of them were moving together now, not drawing nearer but stepping and turning in a kind of accord, like a dance, mocked by their own shadows, accompanied by the tune of the chains and the unearthly sounds that came from the woman. As she turned in this dance, for some moments I saw her more clearly and she was deep-browed and dark-eyed and slenderly made, with straight shoulders—even in the neglect and squalor of that place she was beautiful to look upon. But then I lost the thread of their discourse, I was not versed enough in this language of signs, in the end all was spectacle, as the jailor had promised, the poise of head, movement of hands, sway of body, the pause and pounce of shadows in that inconstant light.

Nor did I understand the ending of it, at least not then. The woman extended her arms, keeping them close together, and showed her open hands to him. He stepped forward and took them in his own and looked down at the palms. So they stood there together for a brief time and then he released her hands and turned away and came toward us, but uncertainly, like one who has looked too long into the light and does not fully see his way.

He spoke no word to me either then or on the way back to the inn. I cast some glances at his face but it was empty of expression. The others, except for Stephen, were already back in the inn yard. It was half dark now and there was a low moon in a bank of cloud. We had to talk of what we had discovered and plan changes to our play and the time for this was short. Martin surprised us by speaking first and breaking the order.

"She is innocent," he said. "At that distance, in that light . . . he could not have seen her face." On his own face was a light, a radiance of intention, like that it had worn when he spoke for Brendan, who had been wordless too. "She was hooded against the weather," he said. He made a swift gesture of drawing a hood close round the face, but he did it in such a way that it did not seem to be against the bite of cold but more in fear of blindness, as at some beauty or dazzlement too strong for eyes, and I remembered the gesture the beggar had made and I knew that Martin was stricken with love for this girl, her face and form were still before him. "She says she was never near the road," he said.

"Says?" I looked at him a moment, then round at the others. "The girl can neither hear nor speak," I said. "We went to the prison to see her. Her father says no money was found there. He was not there that night, he was away from home and there are witnesses to prove it." I told them of my visit to the Weaver, what he had said, what manner of man he was. "He says it was for him they came, not knowing he was from home. He preaches the Last Days and has a following among the people."

"When the Monk held the purse up, it was too late to change the plan." Straw mimed the dismay of the Benedictine, flinging his arms wide, spreading his hands. "O cruel Fortune," he said. "To wait long for opportunity, then find it just at the time the Weaver was not there."

Springer laughed at the mime and after a moment Straw laughed too, but he glanced uneasily about him. "But how did the opportunity come?" he said.

Step by step we were moving toward evil and all of us knew it. Aided and encouraged each by the others, in that barn of twisting shapes and shadows of masks and hanging costumes and weapons that would not wound, to the sound of bells from the church above us and clatter from the yard outside, we were moving toward knowledge of evil.

"So then," Martin said, "having found the purse, the Monk would have to give a reason, explain why he went to the house and took a man with him, and so he said he saw her near the road. It is all lies, she was never there." He looked at us in turn and there was appeal in his look: he was pleading with us to see the girl's innocence. "She was given light," he said, as if to himself. "Perhaps there is someone . . ."

"Martin, they will hang her for all that we can do," Tobias said, and there was pity in his voice, though it was not for the girl.

"The boy had no sign of frost or freezing anywhere about him," Margaret said. "I found Flint again and he found me, and glad enough he was. When Flint came upon Thomas Wells he was stiff and cold but he had no touch of frost. The grass was nipped with it but not a touch on the boy. Flint noticed nothing of this at the time, being taken up by finding the body, but he is quite certain in his memory."

"Good souls," Tobias said, "if the money was taken only to be found again, robbery was not the reason for his killing."

"The Monk and the boy were traveling the same road together at the same time of the day," Springer said in his high, clear voice. "It might be that the Monk questioned him. Thomas Wells would speak the truth to a man in authority, he would show the purse, he would be proud of the trust placed in him . . ."

"So the Monk saw a way to silence the Weaver," Straw said. "That would explain the strangle marks. It is a way of killing that the Weaver might have used."

"She showed me her hands," Martin said. "They are rough with work, rougher than mine." He opened his hands and looked down into them. "Her hands are narrow and the bones small," he said.

None knew how best to answer this because of the daze on his face. And perhaps we were glad to think no further, for the moment at least, about the scene we had created among us: the lonely road, the sense of night not far, the kindly questioning of the Monk, the boy's eagerness to answer . . .

Springer and Straw had gone up to the castle together and played and sung at the gates and in the first forecourt. They had talked to women washing clothes and to the soldiers in the guardhouse inside the gates.

"No one cared so much about the boy's death," Straw said. "They knew of it, but they have a different life up there. The talk was all of the jousting that begins tomorrow and the dancing there will be on Christmas Day."

"Sir Richard and his lady will start the dance as soon as ever they come in from Mass," Springer said. "All the talk was of that, and of the young lord's pining, that is the only son of the house and is named William. They say he is handsome and a very valiant knight and plays well on the viol."

"What pining is that?"

"They do not know what it is. Some say he is wasting for love. He has not been seen for some days but keeps to his room. He has not been out to pace his steed for the tilting or see to his arms, and that is strange for one who all say is passionate for these tourneys and noted for his skill in them —and the more strange as this would be a chance to win honor, with knights from many parts attending."

"Well, the whims of the nobles are of more interest to their scullions than the murder of a child," Martin said, and for the first time since our return his face lost that daze of love and took on a look of bitterness. "Yes," he said, "so he keeps to his room according to his humor. Compared to this lord's indisposition it counts for nothing that she will be hanged on the word of a lying monk." He groaned suddenly and his hand went to shield his face. "She will be hanged," he said.

At this moment, in the midst of our consternation at his suffering, Stephen entered and cursed when he caught his foot against the door. He was drunk and not quite steady on his feet but his voice was clear enough as he greeted us. He had wandered through the town for a while and then gone into an alehouse not far from the church, not for any particular reason it seemed, but only to drink. This was his way when troubled or frightened. He did not think it manly to confess to such feelings and he had not the resource of Springer or Straw or even Tobias, who could find relief in fooling.

While there he had recognized the gravedigger, he who had made Brendan's grave and also that of Thomas Wells. He had spoken to this man and they had drunk together, largely at Stephen's expense, and become confidential.

"The boy's grave was paid for," he said now, sitting with his long legs stretched out before him and his back against the wall. "This gravedigger says that the Lord's steward paid the priest. He says he saw them together. The church door was a little open and they were inside, standing near the font. He saw them talk together, he saw money change hands. Afterward the priest gave him twopence for the work. He dug the grave but he did not see the boy put into the ground."

"How was that?" Springer's eyes were as round as an owl's. "Was it some witchcraft?" he said.

"It was the day before we buried Brendan." Stephen paused and the light glinted on his dark stubble. "The day we came to this cursed place," he said. "He was brought and buried that same evening. When the gravedigger came next morning to finish the digging of Brendan's grave, the boy's was already covered over. He does not know who did this work, or whether the boy was buried in linen or sacking. No one spoke of it to him and he did not venture to ask, having seen the Lord's steward there."

"They fear the Lord's displeasure and with good reason," I said, remembering the two laborers chained in the dungeon. It struck me as very strange and fearful that while we were arriving here, perhaps during our procession through the town, or later when we were giving our Play of Adam, someone had been lowering the boy down in the darkness of night, covering him over, and we all the time unknowing. There had been such haste in the business; Thomas Wells had barely been two days above ground. Who had seen the boy's body? The killer, Flint, the Lord's steward. Surely the mother too had seen it . . .

"He told me something else." Stephen moved his tongue inside his mouth in the manner of the drunken. "In this twelve-month past there have been four boys gone from this town and the country round." He paused and looked before him and again moved his tongue slowly in his mouth. "Four that are known and named," he said. He sat forward and made the orator's gesture of strong statement, right arm extended before him and moved sharply across the body from left to right. "Before that, nothing," he said.

There was a brief silence among us. As before, when Martin had first spoken of making a play out of this murder, a hush seemed to fall over us, in which small noises sounded louder, the movement of creatures in the straw, the breathing of the dog asleep over Tobias's legs. Then Springer leaned forward into the light. "Gone?" he said. "Gone where?"

"Vanished," Stephen said, and his speech had thickened, weariness adding to drunkenness. He raised his hands in the movements of conjuring but did it badly, heavily.

"They will be those the beggar spoke of," I said. "We thought it was only the rambling of his mind."

"This one was found," Martin said. "This one was killed and his purse was taken. The time is not long. We must think how to play it, how to show that she is innocent."

He wanted us not to be led away, he wanted us to think about the one boy, the one play, he wanted us to help him save the woman. And the force of his wish was great with us, also the perversity of this desire for her, which had come on him like an illness.

And so we fell to talking of how it might be done. There

was little enough time, either for talking or practicing. It was decided to begin in the same form as before and to go in the same manner to the point where the woman, still played by Straw, changed to her demon mask. At that moment, when the woman's guilt seemed beyond doubting, Truth would intervene, halt the proceedings and question the players, who would answer as it came to mind, their answers pointing toward the Benedictine. In a third scene, with Truth still in attendance, the true story would be played in mime by Martin as the Monk and Springer as Thomas Wells. Tobias and myself would have the same parts as before. This left no one but Stephen to play Truth and there were some doubts on this score among us, not because he was drunk—it seemed that he often played his usual roles when drunk, God the Father, the King of Persia, the Pope, his air of majesty unimpaired, even enhanced. And he could keep his memory of the lines. But his wits were not thought to be quick enough, whether drunk or sober, for exchanges of speech that were not prepared, and there was a fear he might flounder. However, he was loudly confident of his ability and there was no other way that anyone could see, Tobias not having the stature for it.

"We will do what we can," Martin said. "Tomorrow we shall be better in our parts, we shall learn from our—"

"We will not be here tomorrow." Stephen's voice was loud in that confined place. "By this time tomorrow we will be well on our way to Durham."

"It is too dangerous," Tobias said. "The Lord's confessor, the Lord's steward . . . if it was not the girl who killed him, the one who did it is out there still. The feeling grows on me that he is protected . . ." He looked directly at Martin and again there was something of pity in his look. "We never set out to save the girl, it is you who have taken this idea into your head."

"Yes, it is you, Martin." Straw, as usual, was swept by

the tide of feeling among us. "You are always heedless of us when there is something you want," he said. "We are in danger here. A knife through the hamstring, tac! and our day is over. I have known it done once by a lord who was jealous of another's players."

"We cannot save the girl," I said. "How could we? This Justice that is come to town, perhaps he intends to inquire into the matter."

"What is it to him?" In the passion of being opposed, all color had gone from Martin's face. "What does he care for poor folk?"

"It is her best hope nevertheless."

Springer, the peacemaker, spoke next and he spoke for us all. "We want to leave this town," he said gently to Martin. "We never wanted to come here, it was only for Brendan, and then we spent our money. After tonight we will have money aplenty, more than ever we had together at one time. It is enough, Martin. We are afraid. Every thread draws us deeper into this devil's web." For a moment his clear voice shook a little. "We are afraid," he repeated. "I would be for leaving tonight after the play, if it were not for the dark and the snow."

"Yes, then we would not need to pay that arse-faced innkeeper for the barn again," Stephen said.

And so in the end it was decided among us, with all voting save Martin: we would leave the town as soon as the play was over, travel by torchlight until we came to the cover of woodland, then wait as best we could for the morning light. Martin too had to agree, though there was wretchedness on his face. Whether he would have kept to it is something we were never to learn.

Twelve

WE HAD DECIDED for the inn yard again, because everything was there already and so it saved time. Stephen went to the gate to shout the True Play of Thomas Wells, shortly to begin. And we made ready to do it.

This time we set the curtain posts farther apart to make a greater space for changing and we made it in the middle instead of the corner, with torches set on either side. We would enter into view from the sides so that the people would not be aware of a new player till he came forward into the light. Martin marked the playing space with pegs and a rope, so that none of the people would come on to the ground needed for the players.

All this was done by Martin's invention and design. He set himself to prepare the play with a passion of earnestness greater than I had ever seen in him. He seemed recovered now from his defeat in the voting; and in this seeming recovery, had we but known it, there was mortal danger to us all. That the play and the life outside it were not clearly distinguished in his mind, this we knew; that he hoped still to save the girl we knew too, though we thought it a hope forlorn. But none of us knew how far he would go to save her, what was in his mind to say and do that night, not even those who had been with him longest and knew the extremes of his nature.

I had again the part of Good Counsel in this new play. As before, I had to give my sermon to the boy setting out and I was dressed and ready in my priest's habit and black hat. Peeping through the opening where the curtains joined, I watched the people enter by the gate. Stephen was still shouting the play and Margaret was taking the money, with the innkeeper's man beside her watching everything her hands did. It was useful in some respects to have this fellow, as he knew those who had business there and those who merely said so in order to avoid paying. Also, he barred known troublemakers and the obviously drunken, which Margaret might not have been so well able to do.

The people came in without rowdiness. There was an air of expectation, but it was not altogether the privileged expectation of spectators. It was as though they were gathering for a meeting in which each was expected to play his part.

"They are too quiet," Straw said. He was dressed already in the bonnet and padded gown of the boy's mother. Springer stood beside him in the drab brown of Thomas Wells. "They are coming in as if it were church," he said.

"Stephen should be here now," I said, "if he is to be in time for his scene in the tavern."

We were all nervous, though showing it in different ways. Martin came out to say the Prologue. He was in his usual clothes still and without a mask. He had made up new lines for this, though without saying to us what they were. Perhaps it was only now, with the sound of them filling the yard, that I realized fully what we were embarked on.

"Gentles, we have pondered further.
This grim and grievous deed of murder
Which proven seemed to one and all
And pointed clear to woman's fall . . ."

But there was no time now for second thoughts. There was no time for anything but the playing. We began in the same way as before, with the entrusting of the money and the boy's setting forth. However, Good Counsel had more to do now, my scene of exhortation took up more time, and this was at Martin's direction. "They will be more bound to the play if they are made to wait," he said, "now that the ending is thrown into doubt."

So Tobias, in a demon's mask and carrying a stick with an inflated pig's bladder fastened to the end of it, was also now a part of this scene. Thomas Wells would listen and nod and appear to be persuaded by my words. But then the demon would steal upon me and buffet me with the bladder and I would be distracted into pursuit of the demon and meanwhile the woman would do her mime of pleasures and Thomas Wells would take steps toward her until stayed by some further admonition from me. This made a pattern of movement and gesture very effective and it provoked laughter, which is a welcome thing as saving from silence, but also frightening when there are many laughing together—it is then a sea with strange tides. Players swim in the rise and fall of it and if they lose the mastery they drown.

This laughter sounded near and far, like a shell held to the ear. I moved before the people and tried to do my part. I felt no great ease or confidence in my movements, there had been too little time for practicing beforehand and the timing of things was not easy; the words of the sermon, which I spoke as they came to mind, the gesture of startlement at the touch of the bladder, the breaking off, the turning, the loose-wristed gesture of shooing away, the blundering pursuit. All this had to be done slowly so as to give Straw time for his miming of pleasures. "You must do it as if wearing a loose blindfold," Martin had said to me. "You can see, but not quite clearly. Then you will have an uncertain, groping kind of movement that will slow you and give Straw the time he needs. Also, your blundering will give the demon more seeming of nimbleness."

So I tried to do it in this way. Pretending dimness of sight gave me a distance from the people and I was glad of it, being naked-faced and so seen fully by them. It was not, to speak truly, so much of a pretense: my sight was reduced to a shorter compass; it ended where our shadows ended, as they moved before us; it did not extend to the faces of the people. I turned from the moving shadows to the fluttering light of the torches on the wall, I felt the buffets of the demon, I followed in clumsy pursuit, recovered myself, spoke on a theme from Matthew the Evangelist.

"Thomas Wells, keep you the straight way that leads to salvation, turn not aside. They are voices of Satan that tempt you with soft words and promise of delight. O sinful soul, keep you the narrow way . . ."

Voices came from the people, one more persistent than others, shouting advice to me. Always there are those who think it a great joke to counsel Good Counsel obscenely. "Wrest his stick from him, sir priest, and push it up his arse," this fool shouted and some laughed and some made sounds to hush him. He was taking attention from the play and this can lead to trouble when people have paid to see it.

Thomas Wells was silent and motionless in the center of the space. I gathered myself to speak again, this time on a theme from Job, *The life of man upon earth is a warfare*. But then Straw came forward and swayed before the people in his dance of delights and from behind the sun mask of the Serpent he uttered the unearthly sounds of the dumb woman that he had practiced with Martin, and there fell such a silence over the yard that you could hear the scrape of a shoe on the stones. Facing the people still, Straw tilted his head in the attitude of question and held up his hands, palms outward and fingers held apart. For perhaps ten seconds he remained thus, a long time for a player to hold still. Then from behind the smiling mask came the sounds again and they were drawn out now and wailing in tone so that they seemed like a lamentation of all the dumb things in the world. Then she backed away, and Thomas Wells took his tranced steps toward her, raising his knees in the manner of a dream-walker, but now it was a sorrowing dream, not lustful. I advanced to make the gesture of sorrowful resignation and no voices came from the people at all.

And so we proceeded until that moment when the woman crouches close behind the backs of Avaritia and Pieta and changes masks and shows herself to the people in the horned mask of murder and makes the beast-sign with hooked fingers. The people were still hissing at her when Stephen came forward. He made an imposing figure as he paced between the lights in his white robe and gold crown. He had wanted at first to wear his golden mask but this had seemed wrong to us as it belongs to the part of God the Father. So instead he had painted his face with a thin wash of silver. In his right hand he carried a stave of peeled willow as long as himself. What none of us knew at the time, except Margaret, was that Stephen had drunk more ale while shouting the play and was now quite clouded in his mind.

The first signs of it came soon. He was to have kept to his pacing, with the eyes of the people upon him, while the woman and Avaritia moved out of the light and Tobias came to exchange the mask and cloak of Pieta for the hood of Mankind and emerge again ready to be questioned. But Stephen did not continue long enough for this last to be done, coming to a sudden halt in the center of the space and raising his stave to command attention, so that Tobias had to wait with me inside the curtain until he saw a good moment to come out. However, Stephen's memory for the lines still held and he began without faltering:

> "I am Truth as all men can see.
> With speed I have come to thee,
> Sent by God, out of his majesty . . ."

There was now, however, a disconcerting pause. Not seeing anyone to whom he could put his questions, Stephen made a vague gesture of summons with his stave. "Where is Mankind?" he said, and this was an unwise question, inviting ribald replies. However, none came, so great now was the attention of the people. "Some questions I must put to him," Stephen said, still gesturing.

Tobias came quickly forward, his face shadowed by the hood. "My name is Mankind, I am made of a body and a soul . . ."

With his left hand Stephen made the gesture of accosting. "Goodman, know me for Truth," he said. "Tell us now, where was the boy killed and where found? Speak without fear or favor. Truth is your armor and your stay."

"By the roadside, I hear tell."

There was another pause. Stephen nodded solemnly and raised his stave. It was clear to us that he had lost the thread of the discourse, but fortunately not yet so to the people, who took his silence for majesty. Tobias helped him: "Between the killing and the finding came the dark of night . . ."

Stephen drew himself up. He had remembered: "Goodman, fear not, tell us where Thomas Wells lay between the killing and the finding."

Mankind now moved forward and spoke directly to the people, making at the same time the gesture which accompanies statements of the obvious, palms held up as if testing for rain, then moved sharply outward from the body. "Why, good friends, that is no hard question, he lay by the road."

Thomas Wells himself now spoke for the first time and he too addressed his words to the people, speaking, as agreed beforehand among us, in his own voice and without any gestures or inflections of rhetoric. "Good people, it cannot be so. I must have lain elsewhere. If I had lain there all night there would have been frost on me, but there was none. This we know from the man who found me."

There were voices from somewhere at the back of the yard and then a man called out: "Jack Flint is here. He is a quiet man and he wants me to speak for him. He wants me to say it is true."

The hubbub that followed this died quickly away, leaving silence again among the people. We too for the moment were silent and this was because Truth, having asked these questions, could not think how to go on. After some moments, not finding any other way, he had recourse once again to remembered lines.

> "Truth sets no store by gold or riches
> Nor by emperors, kings, or princes . . ."

Our play might have ended in failure here, but for Martin's readiness. And by this readiness of his he betrayed us and inspired us and brought us to danger of death. Still in the black cloak and hideous mask of Avaritia, he moved forward into the light. Very briefly, and as if merely showing an intention to interrupt, he raised his hand in the sign that means change of discourse. Then he spoke—to us and to the people assembled there:

> "What does Avarice in this place?
> The boy by caitiff hand was slain

But it was not for greed or gain.
So, Avarice, I take leave of you . . ."

As he spoke he undid the fastening of his cloak and let it fall to the ground. With both hands, and slowly, he raised the mask from his face, brought it down to waist height, then cast it from him with the gesture of throwing a quoit. All this took us completely by surprise. It had never been practiced—we had not even spoken of it. And he had given us only the briefest warning. It is my belief that he intended to shock us, along with the people, and take the guard from our tongues. And certainly it had this effect. He made a long pause now, showing himself as plain man. Then he turned toward Stephen, inclining his body forward in the attitude of courtesy.

"How came the child there, Truth, can you expound?
How came this fifth one to be found?"

There lay a hush truly terrible over the inn yard now and over the gallery above. Stephen had no idea how to answer, dulled by ale as he was and moreover too dull of nature to be much shaken by this blow of surprise. He turned his silver face slowly from side to side. "Truth fears no man," he said at last. "Four others there were, to be sure. The gravedigger told me this, whose name is Christopher Hobbs." This said, he lapsed into silence.

Springer's nature was different, however. I saw again the quick rise and fall of his chest as he sought to manage his breathing. He raised his right hand and curled the fingers toward his face as if holding something. "I was carrying a purse of money," he said, and he pitched his voice high, to sound childlike. "That is the difference, good people, that is why the fifth child was found. It was not because of the purse I was killed, but because of it I was found, because the one who killed me wanted the Weaver to be blamed."

Straw came forward. He had removed the murder mask but he still wore the flaxen wig. With movements of his hands and head he mimed the affliction of dumbness. Then he turned with a gesture of appeal toward Mankind who, with the same instinct, had thrust back the hood from his face. We were all without masks now—our sense of the roles we played was shifting, changing.

"The Weaver was from home," Tobias said. "So they took his daughter." He paused, then said in the tone of declamation, "Who took the daughter found the money, who found the money met the boy."

"We met together on the road," Thomas Wells said in his piping voice.

I was standing at the side, away from the light, waiting to come forward to make a sermon on the justice of God, who overthrows the wicked and they are no more, *vertit impios et non sunt.* My heart was beating heavily. It seemed to me that I could see exultation on the faces of the others and also suffering, as if they were looking for release.

"Who met the boy did the deed," Mankind said.

"Where was I taken, whither was I led?" Springer said. "Who knows, let him speak. I was not killed there, by the road. Where did he take me to be killed?" I saw the knowledge of the ordeal of Thomas Wells, which was also the knowledge of evil, deepen on Springer's face. He paused a moment, then spoke in his own voice, forgetting to imitate the pitch of a child: "Why was I taken, if it was not for the purse?"

Martin moved into the center of the space. His face had on it the radiance I recognized. He opened his arms wide.

"That caitiff Monk, where did he hie
By whose hand—"

Whether he was meaning to answer this question himself or would have waited for an answer, I was never to learn.

He was stayed by a great shout from the midst of the people: "The Monk is dead!"

Glancing aside, I saw Margaret standing on the right side of me, near the wall. She had come through the people without my knowing it, so close had been my attention on the play. She was beckoning to me. At the same time I heard some tumult from those round the gate and saw a jostling movement there.

Margaret stood against the rope that marked the limit of the playing space on that side. Her usual sullenness of expression was quite gone. Her face was vivid with the news she had come with. Her mouth was urgent with speech that I could not yet hear. The noise at the far end of the yard was increasing.

"He is dead, the Monk is dead," she said when I was close enough. "They have just come by with him. They are stopped in the press outside the gate."

The movement at the far end of the yard was increasing and a confusion of voices came from there, too many together for me to make out the words. Margaret held to my arm so as not to be jostled aside by the people near us, who were pressing back now, in their turn, toward the gate. "I heard one say he has been hanged," she said, close to my ear.

Still keeping together we let ourselves be carried back. The gate was open and the street outside choked with people who had come out from the yard. It was this that had brought the horses to a halt. We stood in the press while the riders sought to control their mounts, cursing and lashing out at the people so as to make a way through. They wore livery, but it was not that of the Lord. At first, because of the throng, I could see only the upper parts of these riders and the horses' heads and necks. But I moved forward, there was a chance parting of bodies, and I had my first and last sight of Simon Damian as he lay facedown over the back of a mule. I saw his pale scalp and the fringe of his tonsure, I saw his hanging hands as they swayed with the shifting of the mule, scarce two feet above the ground, white hands, waxlike in the torchlight, darkly bruised at the wrists below the sleeves of his shift—he was dressed not in his habit of a Benedictine but in a white shift such as penitents wear when they go in procession.

How long I stood there and saw him thus I do not know. Sights that are momentary can last for ever. When I close my eyes I see him still, the fringe of hair, the dangling hands, the white shift. In the scale that we know it must have been a short time indeed that I stood staring there, before the horseman forced a way through the crowd and the mule moved forward with its burden and was lost to sight.

Margaret had been borne aside and I could see her no more. I turned and came back quickly into the yard. But I could not at once get through to the playing space, being hemmed in all round. The tide of feeling had changed and voices of the people with it. They were shouting now against the players for not having given them the true play, for bringing ill fortune and death to their town. I was afraid among them, but we were so pressed together there near the gate that I do not think they regarded me or knew who I was. All eyes were on the players, who still stood frozen there in the space between the torches. And for some moments, until I came into my proper mind again, I shared this rage against the players, a fury that had risen like a sudden storm at the passing of the dead Monk. I was no longer a player but one of the shouting crowd and in fear and rage I shouted with them. Someone hurled a stone—I saw it strike against the wall. Poor Springer's courage failed at last, he fell to his knees. When I saw this my mind cleared and I knew that the only way to save ourselves was to save the play.

I began to make my way forward as best I could. I heard, or thought I heard, someone shout, "There is one of them, there is the priest." Then Martin broke from stillness, stepped forward until he came to the rope, near enough to touch the front rank of the people, and raised his arms in the gesture of one who surrenders himself, and my heart leapt for his courage and wit, to offer himself to violence and so bring it on himself or disarm it.

He shouted, words not at first audible but then the noise of the people abated and we heard him: "Wait! The Monk is dead but the play is not!"

The shouting rose again like a wave, they were not placated. Still with arms held high, Martin shouted against the shouts: "We knew it! We knew Death would come for him this night!"

It was this lie that saved us. There was muttering still but the shouts died away. Slowly he lowered his arms to his sides and stood thus for some moments without moving. And this stillness also required courage and it pleaded for us more than any gesture could have done. "Do not hurt poor players," he said at last. "Our only wish is to please you. Grant us to finish this our Play of Thomas Wells."

Springer had struggled to his feet and the players stood now in a half circle round Martin, emulating his stillness. I came quickly through the people with no one hindering and stepped into the playing space. An idea had come to me. Plays can be saved by entrances. I was Good Counsel still, I would bring tidings of the death into the play along with my sermon on the theme of God's justice.

And so I did, and fear was mastered in the finding of the words. I moved from side to side, passing between the players and the people, speaking slowly and with solemn gesture. "Now is the Monk sent for, as we all must be, another way to go, to make his reckoning before that Judge whom there is no deceiving. Fair words avail him nothing now, it is no ignorant boy that listens in the dark of a winter day. Before that judgment seat there is no dark, but plenitude of light . . ."

I heard the silence settle over the people and I knew I had done my part to save the play, though knowing no longer where we were going. I kept up my pacing and my speaking so the others would have time to recover their wits and come back into the play. "Too late now, for Simon Damian, for ever too late, the prayer God put into the mouth of Balaam: *Let me die the death of the righteous.* Too late, for ever too late."

The players stood there, keeping the close half circle, motionless still. Fear of the people had stripped them of their roles, they had no resource but stillness. But it was a stillness that had to be broken. "The Monk abused his place," I said, "and God has punished him for it. What says Mankind?"

Tobias spoke, though still without moving. "All earthly power from God doth come," he said.

"That is a true word and it is Truth declares it so," Stephen said, and he turned his silver face toward the people.

Straw was the first to break the circle into which they had drawn themselves to suffer the injury they had thought was coming. He took a single step to the side and said his lines directly to me.

> "Power comes from God in trust to use
> Not the people to abuse . . ."

I had thought Springer would take the longest to recover, forgetting that courage of the fearful which lies in the swiftness of their relief. He moved away from the others and spoke his lines without a tremor.

"Who abuses the people defiles the law
    By use of power to cram his maw . . ."

Stephen now remembered lines from an Interlude he had
played in. They were not much in keeping with the theme of
power abused but they were very much in keeping with
Stephen.

"In England and France our King holds sway
    And so may he do for many a day . . ."

Now Martin, sensing that we were recovered, raised his
hand in greeting to me, at the same time turning it inward at
the wrist in sign of question. "Hail, Good Counsel. Right
glad we are to welcome you. Didst see the dead man close?"

"As close as I see you, brother." I realized now that,
having remained there in the playing space, none of them
yet knew the manner of the Monk's death. "Choked by
rope he made his end," I said.

"His end was like to mine," Springer said, and again he
pitched his voice high to sound like a child.

Mankind was close to the yard wall and the light from
behind glinted on his sparse hairs.

"This Monk did send himself to Hell.
    For him we sound no passing bell . . ."

But at this there rose shouts again. They were not threatening now but they were confused, so it was hard at first to
make out the sense. Then it came to us: "His hands were
tied! His wrists bore the marks of the rope!"

Stephen took a step forward, still holding his stave. He
seemed sobered now, perhaps through the suffering of fear.
"I am Truth, as all can see," he said in his deep voice.
"Those who tied him hanged him. And so he is paid. Who
sheds man's blood, by man will his blood be shed, so it is
written."

But there was something wrong with this. Into my mind there came again a memory of the Monk as he lay over the back of the mule. A white shift, such as penitents wear. Or those being led to execution. They who had tied his hands had dressed him in this fashion. Could the common people have done it? Anyone might have bound him and hanged him, but to dress him thus . . . They had put him in costume, made a player of him, a dancer on the rope. Only those who act in coldness and certainty of power, or who believe God speaks to the God within them . . .

Straw came mincing forward in his robe and wig. "By hanging him they showed me innocent," he said. "Justice gives a voice to the dumb."

We could have ended here. The lines made an ending and they were fitting. We were spent. I could feel the trembling in my knees and Straw, for all his mincing steps, looked close to fainting. But some angel of destruction led Martin further. He was still facing the people and it was to them that he spoke: "It is not justice yet, good people. Why was the Monk hanged? When we know why, we will know who. Everything comes back to the finding of the boy. Thomas Wells was the fifth. He was the one who was found. If the Monk took Thomas Wells is it not likely that he took the others also? But he was only punished for this one who was found. Was it because he had contrived the finding?"

Even now we were drawn to follow, we could not let him stand alone.

"Those who hanged him did it for the finding, not the killing," Springer said. "My killing did not matter to them." There were tears in his voice. A rustle of pity went through the people and some called out that he should not mind because he was in Abraham's bosom.

"Poor soul, they did not want you to be found," Tobias said, and his voice too had the quiver of tears in it. He made the gesture of question. "Who can tell us why?"

"It is because my body bore marks," Springer said. He spoke the words as if prompted. And on his white face there was again the knowledge of the ordeal of Thomas Wells.

"If yours, theirs too were marked, the others." Straw raised his right hand in the sign of counting, thumb tapping at the finger ends. "One-two-three-four-five . . ."

Stephen too had shed tears. There were the marks of them streaking the silver on his face. He flourished with his stave. "Did the mother see the body of her son?" he said.

"No, she did not," a woman shouted from among the people. "She told me they kept her from him."

"Who saw the boy buried?" Martin's voice filled the yard. He looked at us as he asked the question and we answered him together in ragged chorus: "It was the Lord's steward."

Again there came his voice, demanding an answer. "Who did the Monk serve?"

Again with one voice, as though driven, we answered him: "He was the Lord's confessor, he served the noble Lord."

We had moved close together as we answered, obeying some instinct to form ourselves into a single creature with one body and one voice. We were looking across the yard with our backs to the inn. Martin was standing some paces from us; he had placed himself in such a way that he could keep us and the people in his view at the same time. He seemed about to put another question, but I do not think it would have been to us. His face was set and heedless, the eyes fixed. So he had looked when he came from the dumb girl. And so had the girl's father looked when he prophesied the burning of the wicked . . .

Quite suddenly, as we watched him, the expression changed, sharpened into alarm. I heard confused voices from the people and the clatter of armed men behind me. When I turned they were already in the playing space, we were surrounded. They had not come by the gate but through the inn. Some were busy already herding the people out of the yard.

"I am in Holy Orders," I said to the one who seemed to lead them, hoping thereby to avoid this arrest by the laity.

He looked at my stained and dusty habit and smiled a little. "Priest or player," he said, "you will come with the others." Stitched to the breast of his surcoat he wore the leopard and doves of the de Guise. "The woman we do not take, she is not one of the players," he said to the men with him, and I saw Margaret thrust aside.

"Where are you taking us and by what right?" Martin said.

"I am the Lord's steward," he said. He took some moments to look at us, at the poor remnants of our illusion, Straw's red gown, Stephen's streaked face. He was no longer smiling. "You will be guests of the castle," he said. "My Lord desires entertainment."

Thirteen

STRAW WAS GIVEN some time to change and Stephen to wash the silver from his face. The horse and cart, and the grieving dog, were left there. Our masks and costumes we were allowed to take but nothing else. These went onto the back of a mule and it was on muleback that we players traveled the road up to the castle, escorted before and behind, past the church gate where I had been so frightened the day before, when we buried Brendan. There was fear again in my heart now, as we went higher, with the light from our torches ruddy on the snow and the mules slipping a little in the steeper places.

The bridge was down and we clattered over it, past the guardhouse and across the first courtyard with its great wellhead, deserted now, where Springer and Straw had tumbled and sung on that same day and tried to learn more about the murder of Thomas Wells.

On the far side of this we dismounted and were led on foot through another yard, then up stone stairs that went straight at first and afterward in a spiral. And so we came at last to the chamber where they would keep us, a square room flagged with stone, with straw laid over the stone for us to sleep on. The Lord had supped and retired for the night, as had his guests, we were told.

"You are favored," the steward said, and he smiled coldly upon us. "Your room looks down on the tilt yard. You will see something of the jousting tomorrow. Meanwhile, you had better pray to the god of buffoons with particular fervor tonight." The smile died on his face and I knew that he would not forgive us for having brought him into our play. I knew also that he would do what his master ordered and see it as virtue, whatever it was. "You will be brought before the Lord tomorrow at his pleasure," he said, "pray that you please him. You have one with you that can lead you in prayer—he is dressed for the part."

With this he left us. In spite of my anxious state I was plunged into sleep at once almost, so great was my exhaustion; and I think it was the same with the others. But I woke before it was light and lay staring up through the darkness, going over in my mind the events of these last days, the way in which we had been led ever deeper into the circumstances of the boy's death. We had come to the town for Brendan's sake, or so we thought. I remembered how Springer had led us over the brow of the hill and showed us the broad valley and the town lying in it. The wreathing of woodsmoke, the shudder of the bells, that gleam of light in the battlements of the castle . . . The town had seemed to offer itself to us in our need. But it was Death that made this need and sharpened it with Brendan's carrion smell. It was Death that made the appointment for us here. Who then had given us the words of our play? Perhaps we had served Death's purpose now and the play would not be done again. Certainly it was this that we hoped. In the whispered discussion before we slept we had decided to offer the Lord and his guests the Play of the Nativity and the Rage of Herod, as suitable for Christmas, hoping we would be given time beforehand to prepare. In this we deceived ourselves of course. Fear is the patron of self-deceivers but he often comes disguised. I did not know what awaited us as I lay there with the first light breaking through the cracks in the casement; but I knew it would not be at our behest or for our sake that things were done. Into my mind there came the last words we had spoken in our play of Thomas Wells: *He was the Lord's confessor, he served the noble Lord.* They were not the words to end a play with . . .

We heard the horn of the watchman sounding the time of sunrise and not long after a man brought us bread and gruel, for which we were grateful, having eaten nothing since noon of the day before. The door of our room was not kept locked. Outside was a short passage, walled off at one end, with a recess for a privy at the other and beyond that a heavy door locked fast. So on that side there was no means of issuing without someone in attendance. And the window was set high in the wall with a sheer drop below.

From first light we heard hammering and voices from the yard below, preparations for this day of jousting. The sounds accompanied our talking together—we had begun early to talk about the plays we would give before the Lord and his people, allotting the parts among ourselves and deciding on the intervals for dancing and singing, these last being important in Christmas plays. None of us spoke of Thomas Wells, though the plays we were planning concerned the birth of one child and the death of many. By not uttering his name or referring to him in any way we tried to hold off the knowledge of our danger, tried not to think of what had happened, the violent interruption to our play, the seizing of our persons.

Stephen affected to see some cause for complacency in this rough haste. "It is clear that our fame has spread," he said. "They wanted to make sure of us before we left the town." He looked at us and nodded heavily. His eyes were bloodshot, either from drink or his emotion of the night before, when tears had mingled with his silver paint. "It is an honor they have done us," he said.

"Yes, yes," Springer said, eager to find what relief he could from his fears. "They were told to bring us, they are only rough soldiers, they do everything in that way."

Tobias shook his head. He was Mankind still, and voiced the common thought. "A strange way to be honored," he said. "If we had kept to the Play of Adam, do you think we would have been honored thus?"

We were interrupted in this by a blast of trumpets from the yard below and we crowded to the window and threw the casement open to look down, all save Martin who remained as he was, sitting with his back to the wall and staring before him, lost in his thoughts. White doves, startled by the trumpets, flew up past us with a volley of wings and turned in a body above the yard as if stirred together in a great bowl.

It was a scene of great splendor that lay before us. The stands had filled with people while we sat talking and the lists were decked with brightly colored flags from end to end. Mounted and armored but with visors open still, the combatant knights were parading in file the length of the yard and their draped warhorses lifted their heads at the sound of the trumpets and champed on their bridles and their riders drew in the reins and made them prance, with a great sound of jingling. The sky above was cloudless and pale and very distant-seeming. The snow in the yard was churned and trampled and fouled here and there with horse dung, but it was white and firm still and the ridges glittered faintly in the light.

The knights saluted as they rode by and the ladies in the pavilion threw down scarves and sleeves to the ones they favored. Against the white of the snow the beauty of it dazzled my eyes, the bright clothes of the ladies, the fluttering pennants with which the stands and lists were decked, scarlet and silver and blue, the bearings on the shields and breasts of the knights, the glitter of harness and raised lances and crested helmets.

We were the people now, in our turn, they the players. And the play was their own valor and pride. I had seen jousting before, in courtyards and open fields, combats of single champions and melees with a hundred fighting, sometimes with weapons blunted, sometimes not. It is a spectacle very popular with the people now. They crowd to see it with great advantage to pickpockets and whores. But now, perhaps because I had become a player myself, as the trumpets sounded again and the heralds shouted, it came to me for the first time that this was the greatest example of playing that our times afforded. We were players by profession and borrowed roles as seemed fitting. The nobility had only the one but they persisted in it, though denounced by popes and kings for the violence and vainglory of it and the expenditure of money which might have been better spent in maintaining those same popes and kings. The Dominicans preached regularly against it, denouncing these jousts as pagan rites, but all their eloquence was of no avail. The great St. Bernard himself thundered against it and declared anyone killed in a tournament would go directly to Hell, but his words fell on deaf ears. Threats of excommunication had no effect. This was the role that had brought them to wealth and power and they must dress for it and cover themselves in signs and emblems, for what are power and wealth without display?

I was distracted from these thoughts by what, in the language of playing, would be called the Speaking of the Prologue. It falls to the holder of the jousts to announce the rules of combat. He who rose now from his place in the pavilion was the host of these knights and us poor players too, Sir Richard de Guise, and we had our first opportunity to see the man who had caused us to be brought here, on whose pleasure we were waiting. We were too high above to see him clearly. Tall and imposing he was certainly, in the mantle of blue velvet trimmed with ermine that he wore loosely about him. But his face was obscured from us by the brim of his hat and the plume set in it at the side. A long face, seeming narrow because of its length, very pale.

In the hush of respect his rising had occasioned his voice came up to us, clear and deliberate. He was saying things that those listening already knew, but he spoke with solemn dignity, observing his pauses, as Martin might have said. Only blunted lances, or those fitted with a protective coronet, were to be used. If a jousting knight was struck on head or breast he was deemed to have lost the bout. If unhorsed, he forfeited his horse as a prize to the victor. A knight who had fallen was to be helped up only by his own squire wearing his device . . .

His voice went on, sounding sonorously. I thought about his son, the Lord William, and my eyes wandered over the company of knights as they sat astride their chargers, their squires on foot behind. The arms of the de Guise were nowhere to be seen among them. I wondered again what sorrow of love it could be that kept the young lord from the lists. But perhaps he intended to fight later in the day, or on the morrow . . .

My eyes came to rest upon a knight with a helm of very extravagant design. It was in three parts or tiers, the visor being surmounted by a crest of silver filigree and this in turn by a piece in the shape of a cup with fluted sides from which rose the red and white feathers of the plume. It seemed to me that there was something familiar about the squire that stood behind this knight, though the man's back was to me, as was his master's. Then I recognized the arms on the banner of the lance and on the fan crest of the horse, a coiled serpent with bars of blue and silver, and I knew him for the Knight who had stayed at the inn, who had ridden up through the snow beneath his canopy of silk, putting me in fear of the Beast. And it seemed to me entirely in keeping with what I knew of this young knight that he should have paid his armorer a goodly sum to fashion him a helm unlike anyone else's.

Sir Richard came to the end of his discourse, seated himself, and made a sign to the heralds. The trumpets sounded again, and again the doves rose and wheeled above us. The names and lineage of the first combatants were loudly shouted and the devices in their bearings explained at length, the emblems acquired through marriage, the badges denoting seniority of sons, honors gained in battle and by feats of arms, a process taking much time and one that I found tedious. Straw evidently did so too. In spite of his fears—or perhaps in flight from them—he fell to mocking these announcements, opening his hare's eyes wide, gesturing and mouthing with exaggerated courtesy. "Lords and ladies, here is the valiant Springer," he said. "Lord of no acres, victor of no battles but with starvation and that a victory not conclusive. But I wager he can kick higher than any of you, and spin faster on his heels."

Tobias, as was usual with him, took a more sober and practical view. "You see that these champions bear the emblems of their armorers also," he said. "They are paid good fees to do it. The makers of chainmail and plate armor get good custom by these means."

These interruptions were a source of irritation to Stephen, who had been listening intently to the heralds and exclaiming from time to time in admiration and wonder. "Shush," he said. "That is the second son of Sir Henry Bottral. His father married into the Sutton family—you see he has the Sutton arms impaled with his own."

Meanwhile the knights danced their horses and turned their iron masks from side to side and stretched out their silk-clad legs below the hem of their armored skirts for the benefit of the ladies.

Then the visors were closed, the lances leveled, and these first two rode against each other at a slow canter and met with a heavy shock of lance on shield. Both were jolted back in the saddle but neither was unhorsed, so it was a bout with honors even. This encounter, the heart of the play, took less time than saying the first three words of a Miserere.

So it went on through the morning, the trumpets, the shouts, the pounding of hooves slightly muffled by the snow, the resounding clash as the two heavily armed men hurtled together. I was waiting to see the Knight of the canopy and the scarred face. Roger of Yarm was the name the herald gave out. He had fought in the Holy Land and also in Normandy. At his first encounter he bore himself well, changing the tilt of his lance at the last moment so that he struck his adversary on the right shoulder, above the shield, sending him clear over the horse's rump, with his left foot still caught in the stirrup so that the squire had to run forward to free him. In the space of a few moments Roger of Yarm had won the prize of a warhorse, worth fifty livres at least, and he need not have fought again. However, whether led by the desire for glory or gain, in the afternoon he elected to do so and was matched with an older knight, a veteran of Poitiers, who had come from Derby to fight here.

They came to the barrier to salute and Sir Roger's fantastically wrought helm gave him a good ten inches of height more than the other. I have a divining soul, as I have said. As they took their places in the lists I had a premonition of harm and this grew stronger.

The signal was given and they urged their horses forward and brought their lances to the level. How it happened exactly I did not see. The older knight's lance was deflected, but not fully; it slid across the other's shield and rose toward his head. At the last moment, with great address, Sir Roger raised his shield to send the lance point clear beyond him. Had he been wearing a helm of more customary make, this might have succeeded. But the point of the lance, blunted by its coronet, must have hooked in the filigree of the crest and sprung the pins that hinged his visor, so that he received a raking blow along the crown of his head and pitched heavily sideways from his horse to the ground, where he lay without moving.

First to reach him was the squire. Then several followed and among them they bore him away from the lists. There was blood on the snow, where he had fallen.

One further contest there was, then the Lord stood to announce the end of the day's jousting. The afternoon was well advanced, the dark not far away. The knights rode off, with their squires making haste behind them. The Lord crossed the yard and passed inside the castle, followed by his attendants and then the noble guests. Servants came out to take down the cloths of red and gold that draped the pavilions. The daylight ebbed into the snow and there was nothing left now but the bare rails of the lists and barriers, the empty stands, and the darkening stain of blood.

Fourteen

IT WAS NOT until late that he called for us. We had been
brought food again, black puddings and bread and some
thin beer. The candles had been lit and we were stretched
out on the straw.

The steward came for us with two armed men in attendance. We were not taken to the great hall, as we had been
expecting, but through a series of passages narrow and
dimly lit and so into the private apartments that lay beyond
the hall. In passing I glanced down a dark passageway leading off from our own and at the moment I did so a door
opened some way along it, there was a stream of light and a
figure stepped out into this light. It was a woman, a reli-
gious, thickly veiled so that it was not possible to see anything of her face. She was carrying cloths, or perhaps tow-
els, white, draped over the sleeves of her habit. I saw her for
moments only, then the door was closed and the light went
and she passed farther along the passage and disappeared
into the dimness there. But in those moments, while the

door opened and closed and the light came and went and the nun shuffled away into the darkness, there was a stench of decay so strong that I almost choked on it, not the smell of death but of disease, of poisoned tissue and corrupted blood, the rot of the living body. It was a breath I knew, as all who have lived through these times of plague must know and fear it. When that breath is in your nostrils you know it for the smell of the world.

It clamored after us like a creature cheated and grew fainter and died away. We passed through an arched doorway and came into an antechamber, a room with length and breadth enough for the movements of a play but not for holding many people to watch. There was a closet adjoining this with the door set open, and here we found our costumes and masks in a heap on the floor.

In the chamber itself there was a single high-backed chair, with padded rests for the arms, no other furnishing or object of any kind. We stood waiting there under the eye of the steward, while the two guards stood just inside the door with their halberds grounded. It was now that Martin, who had been all that day speechless and dull of eye, seemed to shake himself awake. Whether it was thoughts of the play that roused him so I do not know; playing was the sap of life to him and might have seemed a prospect of relief from the affliction of his love. Perhaps it was simply that he found this yoke of silence too heavy on his neck. Whatever the reason, he raised his head now and looked the steward in the eye. "You are the one who came to see the lad buried," he said. "You paid the priest. Tell us, friend, why the haste?" He paused, still looking closely at the man. Then he said in a voice quickened with contempt, "Or do you not ask yourself even so much?"

At once, with the words, we were under his direction still, even now, as fear grew among us, we were driven to follow him back into the play. Belligerent Stephen raised his head and looked at the steward. Straw uttered his sobbing laugh.

The steward's face had slackened with surprise at being spoken to thus by a man under guard, and moreover a player. "Vagabond scum," he said. "Whipped from parish to parish. Do you dare to take that tone with me? I will have your life for it."

Springer clapped his hands and made his crowing laugh. "Was it you that hanged the Monk?" he said.

"What was his crime?" Tobias said.

We were back in the play again and we fell to questioning him, as if he were in it too, in a part, and so obliged to answer. We were on the edge of despair now, and this took the leash from our tongues. We had been keeping hope alive by clinging to a sense of what is customary. Players are brought sometimes to play in the halls of castles and great houses—this company had after all been sent to do so in Durham. At supper, when the people of the house and their guests are in jovial mood, players and minstrels are often in demand. But when we came into that bare room, with its single waiting chair like a throne of judgment, our poor hope lost all stuffing and collapsed, and we could not keep from knowing the danger we were in.

The steward's hand was on the hilt of his dagger but we knew he would not draw it. In his way he was as helpless as we were. How he would have behaved toward us I do not know. At that moment the door opened, the two soldiers drew themselves up with a crash of their halberd shafts on the stone and the Lord Richard de Guise entered the room.

He had changed his mantle of earlier for a quilted robe of dark red color and he wore a low cap of the same stuff with a black tassel at the side. On his left wrist there sat a hooded falcon. "Set the men outside the door, Henry," he said. "See that they stay within hearing of a shout. Then come back and stand behind my chair."

He looked at us now for the first time, while the steward moved to obey. "So," he said, "you are the players of whom I have heard." He moved his eyes over us slowly. They were pale blue and heavy-lidded, opening to a starkness and fullness of regard difficult to meet. He wore no jewelry or ornament of any kind about him. The cap fitted close at the temples and gave to the long, thin-lipped face a look of bareness and severity. "We shall find out your mettle now," he said.

When he was seated in his chair with the steward in position behind him he moved a hand at us. "I believe they have put your scraps there in the room behind," he said. "You may begin."

Martin stepped forward from among us and made a bow. "My Lord, we are greatly honored, and we will try to please," he said. "With your indulgence, we had in mind to give you the Play of Our Lord's Nativity, as befitting the season."

The long face remained impassive. There was a brief silence, then the voice came, slow and deliberate as ever: "I have not had you brought here to see you make a mock of my religion. It is the play of the dead boy I wish to see. Henry, what was the boy's name?"

"Thomas Wells, my Lord."

"Good, yes, that was it. I wish to see the Play of Thomas Wells."

We had expected no less, but I felt my heart sink. Martin surprised us now and gave us back our spirit. He made the Italian reverence, which players use for the exaggerated courtesy of plotters and false servants, body inclined low, right hand sweeping from left to right in a shallow curve. "As my Lord wishes," he said. One by one we followed him in the reverence, mine executed but poorly, as it is more difficult than might appear and I had never practiced it. Then Martin led us to the room behind, where our things

were, and we dressed for the parts. We could not find anywhere the black murder purse that Tobias had made, so had
to be content with the smaller one in which Martin kept the
common stock. There was no time for talk among us except
for a hasty agreement to do all as before until the departure
of Avaritia and then to have a Messenger arrive with news
of the Monk's death, and to make this death the proof of his
guilt and the symbol of God's justice, without inquiring
further into the authors of it, in other words to end the play
where prudence should have made us end it the day before.
In this lay our only hope, and that a slender one. Of saving
the girl we no longer thought. What none of us knew was
that Martin had decided she could not be saved and so
thought no longer of saving himself.

We followed our plan, keeping to the story we had agreed
on, playing in the stark silence of that room with only the
Lord and his steward for watchers. I think no parts were
ever played before in such a silence as that, before such an
audience. I longed for the clamor of the inn yard and market square again, the laughter and shouts of the people and
the movements of feeling that pass through them. Our steps
fell hollowly in that bare room, we moved back and forth as
if in some slow dance of the newly dead, with the Lord of
the Damned on his spectral throne there, hawk on wrist, his
Minion behind him prompt to do his bidding. Even our
voices seemed unreal to us at first, the very accents of our
quaking souls. But with the setting forth of Thomas Wells
we grew absorbed in the parts, we began to play for ourselves. The mystery of the boy's death was still fresh to us.
This was the third time of playing and we were more perfect
in our parts now, at least in the first half, up to the appearance of Truth, played again by Stephen. There had been no
time for him to paint his face and Pieta had the white mask,
so he was obliged to don a thick mask made of pressed
paper and glue and painted silver. From behind this screen

his voice came slightly muffled but sonorous still. And he
played well, better than I had ever seen him, moving with
great dignity and state, making his rhymes without hesita-
tion.

> "Truth is here for all to see
>   On God's part I come to thee . . ."

In a play with no written words much will depend on
impulse and suggestion. Perhaps it was Stephen, by the
boldness of his playing, who set Martin on his course that
night, made him betray us and put us in mortal terror. At
the point immediately before Avaritia was due to quit the
place Truth spoke directly to the people, as all the Figures
do when they announce their properties. In this case, however, the people were only these two motionless watchers.
Undeterred, Stephen uttered the same lines which had come
straying into his mind when, drunken and distracted, he had
played the part the day before. But now he uttered them
with extraordinary force and conviction, accompanying the
words with the sign of insistence, hand held out with fingers
loosely curled, thumb and first finger touching, little finger
extended.

> "Truth sets no store by gold or riches
>   Nor by emperors, kings, and princes . . ."

It was strange, and also moving, to hear Truth pronounce
these lines with such passion because in his own person, as
we all knew, Stephen set great store by emperors, kings, and
princes, and this immobile figure he was addressing was a
rich and powerful lord, master of lives and land. Stephen
had forgotten himself, he was Truth. And as I stood there, at
the edge of the space, waiting for the moment to come
forward with my sermon on God's justice, I felt a gathering
of tears, even in the midst of the fear that moved like an-

other player among us, to see this servile man rise above himself and boom so boldly behind his mask.

But it was Martin, once again, who changed everything. Truth had asked his questions, Mankind and Thomas Wells had made their first replies. Concealed by the cloaks of Pieta and Avaritia Straw had changed into the murder mask. Still cloaked and masked as Avaritia, Martin moved forward into the center of the space to speak his lines of farewell. He began as before:

"What does Avarice in this place?
The boy by caitiff hand was slain . . ."

But instead of taking leave of Avaritia by disrobing and unmasking, as he had done the day before, remaining there in his own person to question Truth and bring us to a close that might leave some hope of pardon, he made once again that exaggerated reverence, right hand sweeping low. Then he backed away, still bowing to the seated figure, and without any sign to us he disappeared into the room behind.

This departure of Avaritia took us completely by surprise and for some moments we did not know how to go on. Then Mankind found his wits again and asked the question that should have come from Martin:

"How came the child there, Truth, can you expound?
How came this fifth one to be found?"

Stephen had learned from his mistakes of yesterday and he was ready now with his answer. "When Truth pronounces, let no man contradict," he said. "He was taken and laid there because of the purse."

"The one who killed me wanted the Weaver to be blamed," Thomas Wells said in his piping voice. "It was the Monk."

Now was the moment for Tobias to retire, make a quick change into the short cape and feathered hat of the Messenger, and come back with the news of the Monk's hanging. He was already moving toward the changing place when he was brought up short by the reappearance of Martin, still in his red cloak but now in the truly fearsome mask of Superbia, also red except for the curving lines of the mouth and the terrible ridges of the brows, which are painted black.

He signed to Tobias to continue and make speed, then came forward among us and raised his arms at his sides, to the height of his shoulders, with his palms held outward, in the gesture that the Figures make when they present themselves. For some moments he held this posture without speaking, his mask turned toward the seated Lord and the steward behind him. He was giving Tobias time to change. None of us moved. I was standing close to Straw and I could hear the alarmed rustle of his breath through the mouthpiece of the murder mask. Then Martin began his lines of self-description:

> "I am Pride as all can see.
> So I have my rightful sway
> What care I for clerk or lay?"

Now the Messenger came bustling forward in his feathered hat. "Sirs," he said, "I come with news. The Monk is dead, he is hanged."

Eagerly—because this at least we had been prepared for —we tried to fill the space with movement and question, and in this eagerness sometimes two spoke at once and our movements were hasty and clumsy, we obstructed with our bodies the view of those watching. Faults of timing and address, Martin would have called them. We no longer had any notion of where the play was tending, we were drowning in it, we had to snatch words from the air, as drowning people snatch at breath.

Superbia was stalking slowly across the space, stretching

up his neck and making the gestures of kingship and triumphal progress, moving among us like a hideous stranger. Straw made a last effort now to save us and the play, to keep to what we had agreed and bring the story to an ending. He had removed the murder mask and his face was pallid and staring below the garish wig. But he kept to his part, knowing as we all knew that only as players, creatures too low for the Lord's anger, might we still get off with no more than a whipping. So Straw took care with his mincing steps and the movements of his shoulders, and he did it well. He paid no attention to Superbia, still pacing and gesturing behind him. In the center of the space, facing the two who were watching, he made his mime of dumbness, gesturing toward himself with palms turned inward to indicate his affliction, swaying his head for pity. In these moments he was pleading for us all. Then he straightened himself and raised his head and spoke in rhyme to make an ending:

> "Justice has restored my tongue.
> They hanged the Monk that knew his wrong.
> Though I am in prison pent
> Justice shows me innocent . . ."

He would then have bowed, I think, and we would all have followed, but Martin gave us no time. He came forward now, moving up through the midst of us, hissing as he did so—not the snake-hiss but that harsher sound that is made with the teeth closed firmly together. Then he turned to us, right hand raised in the gesture of restraint. His back was toward the watchers. "Pride makes the end, not Justice," he said. "Think you that Pride will suffer an end to be made without him, when he is the master-player of all?" As he spoke, under cover of his body, he made to us the sign of supplication.

We fell back behind him in a half circle, obeying still,

though lost in confusion, that great rule of players that he who is speaking must not be obscured. We were lost, he had scattered our wits and taken our parts away, but we were trapped still in the play, as we were also in that grim room, because in our own persons there was no place for us but the shadow of the gallows tree. It was illusion within illusion, but against all reason we held to it. While Straw was the dumb woman and Springer was Thomas Wells and I was Good Counsel we could not be hauled off and hanged.

Superbia turned now toward the watchers but in such a way that I swallowed on vomit and felt the prickle of sweat in that glacial room. He turned very slowly, taking short steps, head lowered, like some monstrous beast disturbed in repose and turning at last to threaten the disturber. This it was, the threat to the Lord, that gave such a blow to my heart, gave me that foretaste, like a lurch of sickness, of what he was intending.

He was upright again now and facing them. Again he began that stretching of the neck and slow scanning from side to side. He made gestures like a swimmer, thrusting impediment aside. "The master-player of all," he said again. "He stands here and he sits there."

I was standing level with him and I could see the mask in side view and the movement in his throat as he paused. The torch set in the wall behind me flared brighter for these moments and the flame played over the hideous brows and beak of the mask and the shoulders of his cloak. The Lord moved his arm a little, the first movement I had seen him make, and the hawk tilted briefly for balance on the wrist of the leather glove. "I am called by many names," Martin said. "As Pride and Arrogancy, Lordship and Sway. But what care I for names so I keep my dominion?"

He was using a voice not his own. It came through the cruel and bitter mouth of the mask, slow, deliberate, with a sound of metal in it: it was the voice of the Lord. I glanced at the others as they stood there motionless and stiff with no parts to play. Straw and Springer had moved closer together and they were holding hands. And now Superbia spoke again, again in that borrowed voice.

"What care I for one dead boy, or five, or fifteen, so I keep my name and state? Pride it was that held the court, that buried the boy in dark of night, that hanged the traitor Monk in his shift . . ."

It was more than the voice now. To my staggered mind and fevered eyes, as I looked from the mask of Superbia to the face of the seated man, I saw them come closer in resemblance until in that flickering light there was only one face, that of the mask, with its sneering mouth and bulging eyes and jutting brows.

Terror grew with this confusion. Martin in his madness had set himself to flout the judge in the shadow of the judgment seat, to strut before this Lord and simulate his voice, this Lord who held us in his hand. The offense was mortal in itself. But there was more than offense in it. If the threefold arraignment were true, only one meaning could be found to bring it into a relation of logic: Sir Richard de Guise had not wanted the body of Thomas Wells to be seen, because in some way it was marked and he knew this, he knew it because it was into his hands that Simon Damian had delivered the living boy.

How far we would have been permitted to proceed I do not know. I saw Tobias, who was framed strongest of us all and proved it now, come into movement, step forward into the play again, into Martin's view, raising his hand as he did so in the sign of reproach, which is like the sign of cuck-oldry save that the hand is held with the fingers pointing forward. I think he would have tried to save us from wreck even now, by upbraiding Pride for his presumption, but before he could speak there was a disturbance at the door and a young woman came in quickly, bareheaded, wearing a dark cloak over the pale blue silk of her evening gown.

She checked at sight of us, a strange sight no doubt in that silent room, with Pride still making his motions of a swimmer and Tobias with an arm raised stiffly toward him and the rest of us still in our frozen cluster. Then she came forward again to the side of the Lord's chair and he gestured sharply to us and the play stopped.

"I am sorry to disturb you, father," she said. "I did not know where the players had been taken. Sir Roger of Yarm, that was hurt today, is worse, poor soul, he cannot last till morning and the Chaplain nowhere to be found that could administer the Sacrament."

The steward had stepped aside at her approach and the Lord turned toward her in his chair. We took advantage of this to stare reproach at Martin. Straw gestured to him to unmask, but he made no move to do it.

"I am sorry to hear this," the Lord said, in a voice less cold than he had used with us, "but I do not know why you have come to tell me of it now, when I am occupied here."

"It was mother sent me," she said. "She has heard from a maidservant that one of the players is a priest. Perhaps that is the one, who is dressed so."

The eyes of father and daughter were now on me. After a moment the Lord spoke to the steward, who hooked a finger and beckoned me forward. I came to stand before the chair. I was out of the playing space now, I was Nicholas Barber, fugitive priest, sick with fear of death. He raised his head to look at me and the falcon sensed the movement and took a delicate step to the side and it was so quiet in the room that I heard the scratch of talons on the leather.

The Lord had raised the lids of his eyes and his gaze was on me, steady and cold, without curiosity or even hint of question in it. I met this stark gaze for a moment only, then looked down. "Well," he said, "you are dressed for it. Is it true you are a priest?"

"Yes, my Lord, it is true," I said.

"He could come and perform the office," the girl said. "Then I would have him brought back to you here. It would not be long." She hesitated for a moment, then said, "The Knight cannot speak."

The Lord hesitated briefly, raising the ungloved hand to his ear and taking the lobe of it between finger and thumb. Then he nodded. "Perhaps I have seen enough," he said. He looked at the steward. "One man-at-arms goes with him. You and the other man remain with me. Afterward our priest is to be conveyed again to the chamber where they were kept before."

With the lady leading and the man-at-arms clattering behind, we passed from that room, which I was very thankful to do, and went by ways I was too troubled to take much note of toward the place where they had lodged the dying Knight.

He lay in a room without windows on a low bench padded with cushions, with a white quilt drawn up to his chin and white linen binding his head like another helm and candles set on either side. The squire knelt at his feet and he was weeping. There was a low door in the far wall with a table standing near it made with a board and trestles and on this were cloths and a ewer of water and a shallow bowl with the oil in it. A serving woman stood near this and the lady of the house was seated at the bedside. She rose as I entered and moved away without speaking and the squire shifted back to give me room.

The binding came low over the Knight's brow and his face was as pale as the linen. The eyes were brown and long-lashed and they were fixed on something very near or very far. His mouth was a little open and the breath struggled from him. I asked him if he sincerely repented his sins and was ready to make confession, but the eyes did not change and I understood then that the blow had taken away hearing and speech. He seemed very young to me, hardly more than a boy. The skin of his face was smooth, making the scar on his cheek the more strangely incongruous. Death would come in stealth to take the Knight in his youth. And it was near, already his eyes were dwelling on Death.

Absolution I could not give to one who could not signify repentance or speak his sins. I took the oil and blessed it and I began to speak the words for the anointing of the sick and dying and to touch with the Holy Unction his eyes and ears and mouth. He showed no sign of knowing what was done, who only some hours before had dressed in pride for the jousting in the colors of his line and donned his helm of extravagant design, masking for his role as players do. Now he was passing from the playing space with no role left to play but this last one of dying, that comes to all. What there was besides I gave him from my poor store. I said the words he could not hear, I blessed his fading senses. It was my own repentance I gave him, my own hope of Heaven.

The moment of his death was not exactly to be seen, since his breathing had quietened some time before and his eyes had no sight in them. From one moment to the next, with no movement or sound, as I held the Cross before him, his soul took its flight. But the squire knew it and he came forward and knelt by the body, taking my place. And the lady, seeing this, advanced on the other side. The serving woman perhaps did not know he was dead, she had turned to the table, she was wetting a cloth to wipe the sweat of agony from his face. For these few moments no one was looking at me. Outside the door by which I had entered the man-at-arms waited still. But there was this other door.

The hardest thing, once such an impulse has come, is to move slowly. Three steps brought me close enough. I stood with my back to the door and tried it behind me: it was not locked, it gave to my touch. I hesitated no longer but backed from the room onto the narrow landing beyond, closing the door behind me softly. In the last slant of light from the room I was leaving I saw two steps immediately before me and a passage leading away, narrow but straight. There was a latch on the door with a wooden bolt and I pushed this home into the socket. There was no light but I went forward with what speed I could. I had no plan and no real belief I could get away. It was fear that drove me, but for such as myself fear is a potent ally, sharpening the wits and giving wings to the feet.

Fortune aided me, as she had done in the manner of the Knight's death. I reached the end of the passage without hearing any attempt behind me to open the door. There was a turning, then another passage, down which I groped my way. Stairs opened at my feet and I stumbled and almost fell. It was a short stairway—only six steps. I remembered we had been led down two flights of steps when taken before the Lord and so it seemed to me that I might be coming to the ground level of the castle.

And so it proved to be. I emerged from these stairs into the gallery of the Hall, which was still dimly lit with candles and the dying embers in the fireplace, though it was quite deserted. There had been music at supper; the stands of the musicians were still in place along one side of the gallery. A hound slept before the dying fire but took no notice of me as I passed above. There were dishes still on the long table and the Lord's tall chair was pushed back as he had left it, with the benches on either side. I heard voices of serving people from the kitchens but no one came into the Hall as I descended the stairs and crossed the floor.

The moment when I came into the open, which I had been longing to do, was the worst of all, because just as I did so there were voices and moving torches in the courtyard and at first I thought they were in pursuit of me and remained where I was in the shadow of the wall. Then I saw that some were dismounting and among them ladies, and I understood that these were late guests arriving. But I was afraid of being seen and questioned, so I moved away, keeping close to the wall. There was moonlight, enough to see by. I turned down a graveled alley, open to the sky but walled on both sides. I was still without any notion of how to escape from the castle. The main gate was out of the question, the guard would by now be warned.

It was now that Fortune made her boon to me and showed that saying of Terentius, that she favors the valiant, not always to be true. The alley ended in a high wall but there was a gate in it with an open portcullis above. I emerged into a field of trodden snow. Immediately across from me were the railings of the lists and the empty stands: I was in the tilt yard.

However long my life may be, I know that moment will remain with me. The moonlight gleamed on the ridges of the snow and made violet shadows in the hollows. There was the open space to cross, then the posts of the tall pavilion, set close beside the wall.

I crossed the space at a run. I am a good climber as I have said, from earliest days I have been nimble and light of foot —it was this that made Martin incline to take me into the company. It took me not long to reach the roof timbers and swing from there on to the parapet of the wall. It was three times my height or more above ground but I had some skill now in tumbling and the snow had drifted thick against the base. The landing jarred my spine and took the breath from me but no bones were broken. I waited there till I could breathe again, then began to make my way down toward the faint and scattered lights of the town.

Fifteen

IT TOOK ME LONG to reach the town. I kept in cover as far as I could, not using the road much for fear of pursuit—the light was strong enough for a man to be seen moving against the snow. But in the event no pursuit came. Perhaps I was believed to be hiding in some corner of the castle; or perhaps they judged it useless to search in the dark, even with dogs. Whatever the reason I was thankful for it, for my own sake and that of the others, reasoning that while I was at large they were the less likely to come to harm.

I was wet from the waist down and chilled and exhausted when I came to the inn, hardly able to keep from staggering in my walk. The yard lay deserted. There was no sound anywhere, but one of the upstairs rooms showed a crack of light between the shutters. It was the room at the end of the gallery, the Justice's. The inn door was open still. I mounted the stairs and went softly down the passage to the end room. Light came from under the door. I stood there for some moments, listening first to my own loud heart and then to a voice from within the room that droned and paused and resumed again. I gathered what courage I had and rapped with my knuckles against the panel.

I heard the voice break off. Then the door was opened and a man of middle years stood at the threshold, a thin man, sharp of feature, dressed in a black coat such as attorneys wear. His eyes ran over me, my shaven head, the wet and bedraggled skirts of my habit. "What do you seek?" he said, in no very friendly manner. A larger man stood beyond him, in the middle of the room.

"I would speak with the Justice," I said.

"On what business?"

"It is about the murdered boy," I said. "I am a priest . . . I am one of the players."

"It is late," he said. "The Lord Justice is occupied. Will it not keep until the morning?"

"Let him come in."

It was not said loudly, but the voice was of one accustomed to command. The man at the door moved aside and I went into the room. There was a desk with scrolls upon it and a good fire burning in the grate. Tall candles burned in a triple-headed brass sconce and they had the clear flame that only comes from good tallow. This was far beyond the means of the inn to provide, as were also the red and gold damask hangings on the walls. Facing me was a man of corpulent body and good height, dressed in a black skullcap and a black velvet mantle held at the neck with a jeweled pin. "So," he said, "a priest who is a player is not so infrequent, especially among priests who get advancement, eh, Thomas?"

"No, sir."

"A player who is also a priest, I grant you, that is rarer. This is my secretary, and a very promising advocate. What is your name?"

I told him but I do not think he took note of it, not then. He looked at me more closely as I spoke and his face changed. "Set a chair for him," he said. "Here by the fire. Give him a glass of that red wine we brought with us."

And in truth I think he saved me from fainting in the sudden warmth and brightness of that room.

"Such wine you will not find in a place like this," he said, watching me drink. "I saw the play from my window here. It was very well done—far beyond the common. Your master-player is a man greatly gifted."

"Better for us had he been less so," I said.

"Indeed?" He mused for some moments, looking toward the fire. His face was heavy and hung in folds, as if too much flesh had piled on the bone; but the brow was high and the mouth was firmly molded. The eyes, when he looked up at me, were considering and cold—also, as it seemed to me, in some way sad, as possessing knowledge not much prized. "What brings you here?" he said, and he signed to the secretary to replenish my glass.

At this I told him all that had happened, trying to keep things in the order of their occurring, which was not easy in my weary state, would not have been easy whatever my state, when so much had depended on accident and surmise.

I told him how Brendan's death had brought me into the company and then brought the company to the town. I told him of our failure with the Play of Adam and our desperate need for money so as to continue on our way to Durham. I told him of Martin's idea for making a play out of the murdering of Thomas Wells, which was something that belonged to the town.

"We did not doubt at first, when we began, that the girl was guilty," I said. "There was no reason to think otherwise, she had been tried and condemned for it. But the more we discovered, the more difficult it was to go on believing this. And it was not only the things that we learned by inquiry." I faltered now, coming to the part least likely to be believed. His eyes rested on me with the same expression, attentive and cold but not unkind. "We learned through the play," I said. "We learned through the parts we were given. It is something not easy to explain. I am new to playing but it has seemed to me like dreaming. The player is himself and another. When he looks at the others in the play he knows he is part of their dreaming just as they are part of his. From this come thoughts and words that outside the play he would not readily admit to his mind."

"I see, yes," he said. "And as you played the murder . . ."

"It pointed always away from the girl, first to the Benedictine, because he had lied."

I was beginning to tell him of these lies but he held up a hand. "I have read the deposition of the Benedictine," he said.

It was the first sign he gave that he had occupied himself with the matter and my heart rose at it. "But then he was hanged," I said. "They dressed him in a penitent's shift and tied his hands and hanged him. And we thought it must be a punishment because he caused this one to be found. But only the powerful would punish in that way, those who hold their power from God or the King."

"We servants of the Crown would say it is the self same thing, eh, Thomas?"

"Yes, sir."

He had smiled a little, saying this, and again I saw some quality of sadness in his face, something that I did not think had always been there, that had come with the years of good living and the authority of his office. "So then," he said, "the Monk took the body of Thomas Wells, after someone else had killed him, and laid it there on the road. Then that someone else, or another, killed the Monk. Did you not ask yourselves why he chose that particular time to bring back the boy's body? Why did he wait so long? It was a dangerous time, was it not? It must have been getting light. In fact the man Flint found the boy not much after."

"Perhaps he was not killed until then."

He shook his head. "The boy was taken in the afternoon, as it grew dark. The one he was taken to would have been waiting, no doubt impatiently. It is not likely that Thomas Wells was strangled as an afterthought. Dawn is a common time for killing oneself, but not others. Unless it be by Royal Warrant, eh, Thomas? Give him some more wine, half a glass only—he will need to keep his wits about him yet."

"Then there was the haste of it," I said. "And the steward came and paid the priest and saw the boy buried. It began to seem—"

I stopped short with a sudden fear, looking at the fleshy, keen-eyed face before me. The wine was loosening my tongue, but there was danger in such frankness. Had I escaped from one trap only to fall into another? "We meant no harm, it was only to make a play," I said. "We were led to it, step by step."

"There is nothing to fear," he said. "I give you my word on it. I will require nothing from you, save only this account."

I could only hope that this was true. I had gone too far now to retract or fall silent. "Then Martin was stricken with love for the girl," I said. "It was beyond all reason, he saw her only once."

I told him then of our arrest and of how we had been kept for a night and a day, then taken before the Lord and made to do the play, but in a private chamber and before the Lord and steward only, and how Martin had betrayed us.

"You will be the first players to have set foot in Sir Richard's private apartments," he said. "He is fond of music, they say, but not of shows and plays. He is a man of austere life." The Justice spoke with pity almost, as if it concerned some aberration of the spirit.

"Well," I said, "the chamber was austere enough, there was nothing in it but a chair. There was nothing to remark anywhere but the smell of plague as we went by."

I had said this as an afterthought but he raised his head at it and fixed his eyes on my face. "Plague? Are you sure?"

"I am sure, yes. It is not a smell like any other. Once you have known it, you will know it always again. It came from a room that we passed on the way."

"Perhaps the one within was gone already to his Judge?"

"I do not think so." I sought to remember, not as myself thinking the matter important, but because of his very evident interest in it. There was the short passage, the suddenly opened door, the veiled and hooded sister with the white cloths draping the sleeves of her habit, the smell of death-in-life that followed us. "It was only the impression of a moment, as we went by," I said. "I think the one in the room was still being cared for in some fashion."

He was silent for a long moment. Then he nodded slightly and it seemed indifferently and looked away. "Yes, I see," he said. "Picture it, Thomas. This player come from nowhere, puts on the mask of Superbia, and gives him back look for look in his own chamber, Sir Richard de Guise, one of the strongest barons north of the Humber, with lands that go east from here as far as Whitby, who dispenses his own justice, not the King's, and has his own army and his own court and his own prison."

"The man must be mad," the secretary said.

"Madness you call it?" His eyes returned to me. "I had thought love would make a man want to preserve his life, not throw it away."

"He is a man who goes to extremes. Besides, he had lost hope that the girl could be saved. He did not know . . ." Here I was obliged to make a pause and master myself, as gratitude threatened me with tears. "None of us knew," I said, "that you had come to administer the King's justice and set this foul wrong right."

And now his eyes were full upon me, narrowed in a scrutiny that seemed half-amused, half-incredulous. "The King's justice," he said. "Do you know what it is, the King's justice? Do you think I would leave his business in York and come these weary miles in this weather, to this wretched inn where I am served food not fit for the swill tub, for the sake of a dead serf and a dumb goatgirl?"

"I did not think there could be other reason for your coming. I thought—"

"You thought I was one of your company, one of the players, somewhat belated, come to put on the mask of Justitia in your True Play of Thomas Wells. There was the Monk and the Lord and the Weaver and the Knight. And now the Justice, who sets all things right in the end. But I am in a different play. What did you say was your name?"

"Nicholas Barber."

"How old are you, Nicholas?"

"This is my twenty-third winter, sir," I said.

He sat back in his chair and looked at me for a moment or two, then shook his head. "I have no sons, only daughters," he said. "But if I had one such as you I would be concerned lest simplicity bring him to folly and thence to grief. You are at the stage of folly already, are you not? You are outside your diocese without license, you have joined a company of players."

"Yes," I said, "it is true."

"What led you to do so?" He was looking closely at me still, but with an air now of simple curiosity which was somehow more disturbing to me than that former derisive incredulity. "You had a certain position," he said. "You are lettered. You could have hoped for advancement."

"I am, or was, one of the sub-deacons at the Cathedral of

Lincoln," I said. "I was set to transcribe Pilato's Homer for a benefactor, a work extremely tedious and verbose. It was the month of May, the birds were singing outside my window and the hawthorn was breaking into flower."

"So simple as that?" He glanced aside. "No more than an impulse." His eyes moved over the rich hangings on the walls, the bright blaze of the fire, the silent and attentive secretary. "Thomas has never done a thing like that, have you, Thomas?"

"No, sir."

"Thomas will sit on the King's Bench someday." He looked at me again. "I have never done a thing like that either. I have studied and worked for one part only. If such impulse had come to me I would have taken it for sickness."

He fell silent and for some moments there was no sound in the room but the whisper of the fire. Then he stirred, as if waking. "Thomas and I have some private business to conclude," he said. "I will ask you to wait elsewhere for a brief while. Then we will go on a short journey together. But first I will tell you something about the King's justice, though I do not hope to lessen your simplicity thereby. For a dozen years or more, since I first came close in counsel to the King, we have had trouble with this stiff-necked de Guise. He keeps men under arms in numbers more than needful and they are unruly and oppressive and threaten the peace of the realm, and the dues that are the King's prerogative go to paying their wages. He combines with others to maintain the right of the lords, as peers of the realm, to pronounce judgment on their fellows, thus denying the King's right of impeachment. He takes the law into his hands. Only Royal Commissioners have the power to try cases of felony in the shires, and all fines and expropriations should go to the Royal Exchequer, yet this Lord arrogates such powers of trial to his Sheriff's court and all the moneys go into his coffers."

He paused, with a compression of the lips. "You see?" he said. "No way but force with such a man. And this is not a time for force, with the loyalties of the people uncertain and a Commons always ready to cry tyranny. But I kept him in my view, there was one in his following who reported to me. Then, a year ago, we began to hear stories of disappearing children, those you know of and others, vagabond children about the town, parentless children who came to beg at the castle gates. Always boys. And now this case of Thomas Wells, the one who was found, and finally a path that led to the house of de Guise."

He paused, smiling, and stretched out white hands to the fire as if cherishing still the wondrous warmth of that opportunity and the gems of his fingers flashed in the firelight. "I have looked very carefully at this case," he said. "And I know the truth of it now."

"And now you will bring him to justice and serve the King's cause at the same time."

He shook his head and smiled again. "I see well that you have been put to copy the wrong books," he said. "Do you think he would meekly consent to be tried? Justice is less easily applied to the strong than to the defenseless. It is the fame of his house that concerns him most. We are fortunate in the nature of the crime."

"Fortunate? Thomas Wells would not say so, if he had a voice."

The smile faded and his eyes narrowed in the heavy face as he looked at me and I understood what it might mean to be an obstacle in the path of such a man as this. "What we cannot change we do not waste time over unless we can make use of it," he said. "It is time you learned that, Nicholas Barber. The manner of the boy's death is something we can make use of. There are mortal sins and mortal sins. Some might add luster to a pride like his. But not, I think, the sin of sodomy. No, I will talk to him and he will listen, and he will go on listening as long as he lives." He paused for a moment and his expression softened a little. "One thing only was puzzling me and you have shed full light on that. I am grateful to you."

"How did I do so?"

"Later you will know it. You will wait for us now some little while. Then we will take a ride together, and I promise you enlightenment at the end."

"To the castle?"

He rose to his feet and stood looking down at me from his greater height. "Not to the castle," he said.

I was moving toward the door when he spoke again. "You will come to no harm. Wait for me below, do not run away. After this journey it will lie in my power to deliver the girl from prison into your keeping."

"And the others, what of them?"

"Yes," he said, "them too. Have no fear, it will not be too late. Yesterday when you were taken, I sent some lines to Sir Richard, enough to give him pause. That is what I can do for your friends. For you I can put in a word with the Bishop of Lincoln if you desire to return."

I would have thanked him but he waved a hand in dismissal and the secretary came forward to show me from the room. I went down the stairs again and out into the yard. Moving quietly and keeping near the wall I made my way to the barn and tried the door: it was chained on the inside. I rattled the door against the chain, not too loudly. There came the sound of a dog from inside, something between a bark and a whine. Then I heard Margaret's voice, thick with sleep, asking who was there.

"It is me, Nicholas," I said, speaking close to the door.

After some moments I heard the key turn and the door was opened wide enough to let me in. Margaret had lit a candle and she held it in her hand. The light was cast upward over her broad cheekbones and the tangles of her hair.

"Well, you are back," she said. "I was going to wait until the morning."

I did not understand what she intended by this but before I could make any reply she gave me the candle to hold and turned and burrowed briefly in the straw. When she stood again she was holding the box in which we kept our takings. "Another night in this piss-hole I will not stay," she said. "There are sixteen shillings and fourpence in this box. That is what is left of our takings. I have had to pay two nights' lodging here. That stinkard would have taken it in kind but I cannot abide him. Hold up the candle, Nicholas, and I will count it out. Half I keep for myself, who do not belong to this company and never did, nor any other."

She began to count the coins out into my palm. No word of sympathy for my weary state or inquiry about the others.

"Margaret, we did not abandon you," I said. "We had no choice but to go."

"It is not that," she said. "Wait, or I will lose my count."

The money was all in pennies and my hand could not hold so much. "You can put it in this," she said, and she found for me the black murder purse, which I had seen last when Martin held it up before the people at full stretch of his arms, as if it were the Host. "I kept it ready," Margaret said.

When it was all counted out she sighed and nodded and turned to put her box again in its place under the straw. "I take half in payment," she said. "Other payment I had none. I knew I would be given no share in the playing, but I did things that were needed and no one else could do them and I thought I would have my place in the company, but no place was given to me, except only what served you. I did not want to think it before, but when the soldiers came and took you and did not even bother to take me I was made to think of it and I knew I counted for nothing."

"With them, no."

"With you either," she said very simply, as if there could be no argument.

It seemed to me strange and illogical, and belonging to the unreasonable nature of women, that Margaret should so resent being spared the danger of death and moreover should blame us for it, who had been placed in that danger. "The others are held still, they are in the castle," I said. "They are in danger of their lives."

"I do not want to hear of it," she said. "They are the players, the play is theirs."

"Where will you go?"

"I will go to Flint. He came at noon today to ask for me. The twice we were together pleased him. He wants to take me into his house. He will take the dog too. He says it is young enough still to be trained for sheep. The innkeeper says he will look to the horse, he is hoping that no one comes back to claim it."

I did not think that the dog would come up to Flint's expectations and I was not altogether sure that Margaret would, but I naturally kept silent on this score. "Well," I said, "I wish you good fortune with all my heart."

At this she smiled a little but without much softening and after a moment she came and kissed me. "Go back to your Bishop, you were best," she said.

"Well, that is doubtful," I said. "As for this question of being admitted to the company and having a part to play, you can take comfort from the story of the Devil and Player, do you know the one?"

She shook her head and yawned, in a manner not encouraging. Nevertheless, I persisted, because I thought there might be consolation in it for her.

"It took place before there were players, if we can imagine such a time. The Devil was casting about the world and he came upon a man of very virtuous life and sought to tempt him. He tried all manner of blandishment, the lusts of the flesh, the treasures of the world, fame and dominion. All of these the man steadfastly rejected. The Devil was at his wit's end and could think of nothing more but to offer to make him a player. The man saw no harm in this and agreed and so he lost the bout and his soul was forfeit because a player borrows bits and pieces from the souls of others and in this pastime his own soul loosens and slips away from him and it is an easy matter for the Devil to scoop it up. And this has been the case with players ever since."

Margaret's response to this story confirmed me in my view that women have no head for abstract thought.

"If Stephen escapes hanging," she said, "tell him Flint is big and strong and has both his thumbs and plenty of gristle in them."

I promised to do this and she lay down again to sleep. I sat on the straw with my back to the wall and tried to think of what the Justice had told me. The Lord must already have had the message, perhaps it was somewhere about him while he sat watching our play. Martin had mocked him in the mask of Superbia and sought to bring him into the Play of Thomas Wells. But that note, which I had not read and never would, had forced on him a part in another play, that in which the Justice was a player and the King also, a larger play in which the suffering of the innocent was of no importance except as a counter to bargain with. And as my eyes grew heavy with sleep I wondered if there were not some larger play still, in which Kings and Emperors and Popes, though thinking they are in the center of the space, are really only in the margin . . .

Sixteen

I WAS ROUSED by a voice at the barn door, Margaret too, but I rose and went out quickly before she was fully awake. There were a dozen men in the yard, several of them clad in mail and armed. The Justice was in the midst, with a group of hooded men about him, among whom I made out the lantern jaws of the secretary. These were on horseback but there were others with mules and two of them had spades slung across the saddles and coils of rope. When I saw this I began to suspect the nature of this journey. But there was no time for question: a mule was ready saddled for me and I mounted.

The moon was high now, riding in a clear sky, and there was light enough as we rode through the town, though several carried unkindled torches. We took the road that led upward to the church, riding now not so much together, with those of us on muleback strung out behind and the open country on either side. In the hollows and lower slopes of the land and up against the stone walls that ran across, the snow had drifted and heaped to make shapes that seemed unfinished in that pale radiance of moonlight, shapes of animals and men not yet formed into being, with blunt heads and limbs, folds where eyes might one day be, pocks and dimples waiting to be molded. The snow was softening at last, the hooves of the mounts in front cast up a dust of white that rose to their knees.

Moonlight silvered the grass of the churchyard and glinted on the snow that lay over Brendan's grave, so newly dug but seeming already to belong to a time remote. The boy's tarred cross still stood there, marking the small plot where his body lay, and it was here they began digging, using at first a long-handled pick as the ground beneath the snow was still frozen hard. And now the torches were lit and the reddish light of burning hemp engorged the light of the moon, so that beyond the flames there was only darkness.

I stood within the circle of the torchlight, on the edge of it, watching. The earth below the frosted surface was loose-packed still and made no resistance. Some muttered words were exchanged between the Justice and one of the hooded men who stood close beside him. After this there was only the waiting and the torchlight and no sound but the scrape of the spades and the spill of earth.

Then came the striking of metal on wood and a man got down into that narrow space with ropes and the coffin was brought up and laid near the grave and the same man forced open the lid.

My impressions of what followed were confused and they have always remained so in memory. The men who had been digging fell back. Two of those who had been standing with the Justice moved forward and with them one bearing a torch. I saw now, as the light fell on them, that both these men wore masks of some dark stuff over the lower part of their faces, covering the nose and mouth. And as they leaned down to the coffin I saw that they wore dark gloves. There was a smell like that which had come from the chamber in the castle, but fainter. The two who were hooded and masked were busy about the body but I did not see clearly what they did. Then the Justice turned and looked toward me and motioned me to join him. He was nearer to the body but not so close that he could have touched it. I came as he bade me and looked at what they were doing and I saw the true face of Thomas Wells, who had worn Springer's face before and then the cloth face of the effigy with holes for eyes where the straw poked through. And this face was less real than either, it was lost in death. The smell was stronger now. They turned his naked body this way and that and his arms and legs trailed in the snow.

In the circle of the torchlight there were only those busy with the body, and the Justice and I. The men-at-arms had remained some way off where the horses were tethered and the others had been sent to join them there. One of the hooded men looked up at the Justice and spoke quietly in a voice that was muffled by the mask. "There was an act of sodomy, beyond any doubt, and violent enough. The body was not washed, or washed only hastily—there are traces of blood still. And there are marks of strangulation. But his neck is broken and that is how he died. I would say that he was strangled half to death—probably while the act was taking place—then had his neck broken in a single wrench. Somebody strong it would need to be."

He was silent for a moment, looking up toward us through the light. Then he said, "He would have died anyway, quite soon. You were right, my Lord Justice. He was infected. Look here." He took the right wrist of Thomas Wells and raised his arm toward us. "Bring the light closer," he said to the one with the torch.

In the hollow of the armpit there was a black swelling the size of a hen's egg and the skin round this was broken where some viscid substance had oozed when the body had life, and formed a dark crust now. Particles of melting snow lay on his poor face and chest and made a wet stain like a spreading of this discharge.

"It is there also in the right groin, though smaller," the hooded man said. "You would need to come closer to see it."

"I have seen enough." The Justice turned away. "Make sure the poor lad is shrouded and laid properly in earth again," he said over his shoulder, and he moved away taking me with him.

We rode back together, he managing his horse to keep beside me and his people staying behind. And as we went he told me what I still needed to know for my full understanding. "The Monk it was who procured the boys," he said. "There will be some mire or cesspit in the castle grounds or some secret place in the cellars below where he hid the bodies after. No doubt a search would discover it, but we shall not need to go so far."

"Why should a man do such evil? What could be the recompense?"

"These are questions without great meaning in them, Nicholas. Wickedness is too common in the world for us to think much of why and wherefore. It is more natural to ask about the rarer thing and wonder why people sometimes do good. Perhaps he liked to watch it. Perhaps he was paid. Perhaps he wanted that power that comes from being necessary to the powerful."

I did not in my heart believe in such preponderance of wickedness and I do not still, except sometimes when my spirits are low. "Well," I said, "the one he served had him hanged for his pains."

"He was hanged for his crimes, and to keep him from speaking. And it was not done by the one he served. The one he served was already dying."

For a moment, as we rode along, in a light less certain now, with the clouding of the moon, there came into my mind that last, strangely driven chorus of ours in the True Play of Thomas Wells: *He was the Lord's confessor, he served the noble Lord* . . . "Of course," I said. "I see it now. It was the young lord, the son. Simon Damian was the Lord's confessor, yes, but it was the son that he served. The father must have discovered it somehow, or perhaps he knew it already in the way things are known but not admitted to the mind."

"It may be that the young man confessed it when he knew he was going to die," the Justice said. "William de Guise, favorite of the ladies, only son of the house, flower of chivalry."

"That is why he kept to his room. That is why he was not at the jousting."

"You see," the Justice said, "there were two things that made Thomas Wells different from the others: he was carrying a purse of money and he was recently infected with the plague. Perhaps he felt ill already and rested on the way, and that was why he was still on the road as dark came down. The Monk knew about the purse. But no one knew of the plague marks until William de Guise, pride of his father's heart, had snapped the boy's neck. Then, with his lust sated, he would have been at more leisure to notice. Once he knew it he would have not touched the boy again. No one would. So he lay there through the night. Then Simon Damian had his idea. He waited for as long as he dared. For twelve hours after death the disease is contagious still, or so at least the people believe, though I have heard doctors give it out as longer. It was a question of getting the body dressed again and left there on the road before daylight—he could not risk being seen. All this was obscure to me until tonight, until you told me of the plague stench in the private apartments of the castle."

After this we went on for some time in silence. I was thinking that the Monk must have hated the Weaver greatly to have risked so much: not merely the anger of his master but the foul breath of the disease. But of course he must have known that his role of bawd was over. Perhaps he was searching for another. To the one whose savage lusts he had fed, and to whom in the end he had fed pestilence and death, no role could be given, no mask more terrible than his own face.

"He is no more now than an evil smell," the Justice said, as if divining the current of my thoughts. "No one lives longer than six days after the appearance of the first symptoms. It is six days now since the Monk set out with the dead boy. It must have been just at this time in the morning. See, it will soon be light."

Ahead of us, above the roofs and chimneys of the town, there were the first livid streaks of a new day. We were coming now to the street where the prison was. One question remained, greatly troubling to my soul. I remembered Stephen's words and his gesture of an orator as he sat drunken in the barn, his long legs stretched before him. *Before that, nothing . . .*

"Why only now, in these last months?" I said. "Why not before? What shape of Hell could have visited the young lord when he was grown already to manhood?"

The Justice glanced down on me. His face was deeply shadowed by the hood he wore and I could make out no expression on it. "Always you ask the why of things," he said. "The seed was there. There is a growing time for every plant and it may be long but the flowers open quickly when they come. And these had sun and water from the Monk, no doubt a subtle gardener enough."

We came to the prison door and one of the men-at-arms struck on it with a mailed fist. The turnkey was grumbling as he peered through the grid but he fell silent when he saw with whom he had to deal and he opened to us and bowed low. I waited alone there, in the alley. There were others that remained outside with the horses but I kept apart from them. The reply of the Justice had not satisfied my mind. I wondered who might have planted such a seed and when it had been done. I thought it might have been done by Satan at a time when the Lord William was sleeping or when he was too young to know it, perhaps even younger than this Thomas Wells whom he had tortured and killed . . .

When they came forth again the girl was walking free among them. "She is in your keeping now," the Justice said and he led her to me and placed her hand in mine. But it was not me she had to thank and she knew it. She made no sound but when the Justice, assisted by one of his people, had climbed back into the saddle, she moved away from me and went to him and reached for his hand to kiss. It was the first gesture of her freedom. He smiled down over her lowered head, the first smile without irony I had seen on his face. And I could not help thinking of the strangeness of it, that he should garner this gratitude and take it for his due— as I could see from his face that he did—when her life mattered nothing to him, when she had escaped hanging by merest chance, as an afterthought, a casual change of discourse in the play.

"This is an example of the King's justice," I said. "What of God's?"

He turned his horse, smiling still. "That is more difficult to understand," he said. "It is not the King that visits us with pestilence. You have been useful to me, Nicholas Barber, and I would help you if I could. Have you thought more of my offer to restore you to the good graces of your Bishop?"

In truth I had not thought much of it, having had little time for reflection. But as I looked up at him in this first light of day I knew what my answer should be, and it was what the Play of Thomas Wells had taught me. I would not go to Lincoln again, unless it was as a player. I knew little of the world, as the Justice had seen, but I knew that we can lose ourselves in the parts we play and if this continues too long we will not find our way back again. When I was a sub-deacon transcribing Pilato's Homer for a noble patron, I had thought I was serving God but I was only acting at the direction of the Bishop, who is the master-actor for all that company of the Cathedral. I was in the part of a hired scribe but I did not know this, I thought it was my true self. God is not served by self-deceiving. The impulse to run away had not been folly but the wisdom of my heart. I would be a player and I would try to guard my soul, unlike the Player in the fable. And I would not again be trapped in a part. "I am grateful, my Lord Justice," I said, "but I will remain a player now."

The Justice nodded. He was no longer smiling. His expression was watchful and cold and a little sad, as it had been when first I began telling my story to him. "The choice is yours to make," he said. "Go back now to the inn and wait there. Your friends will join you later today—you have my assurance on it. I must go now and have my talk with Sir Richard de Guise."

He nodded again and moved away, his people falling in behind him. We watched them until their forms were lost in the uncertain light. The girl raised her hands and tried to restore some order to the wildness of her hair. And I wondered whether Martin would continue to love her, now that she was no longer chained.

ABOUT THE AUTHOR

Barry Unsworth's previous novels include *Sacred Hunger*, winner of the 1992 Booker Prize, as well as *Mooncranker's Gift*, *The Rage of the Vulture*, *Stone Virgin*, and *Pascali's Island* (U.S. title: *The Idol Hunter*), which served as the basis for a film. A Fellow of the Royal Society of Literature, he currently lives in Italy.